Born in London in 1973, David Horan and his twin brother are the youngest of a large family.

David grew up in several different places in North London and went to school in Finchley.

Whilst living in the Golders Green area for many years, David attended various colleges and Thames Valley University.

David has a great interest in the Natural World and conservation. David has been writing for 20 years, screenplays for films and theatre projects, but this is his first children's novel.

To my beloved mum, always in my heart.

David Horan

ANDREW AND THE MIDNIGHT APE

AUSTIN MACAULEY PUBLISHERS™

LONDON • CAMBRIDGE • NEW YORK • SHARJAH

A CIP catalogue record for this title is available from the British Library.

ISBN 9781398430396 (Paperback)
ISBN 9781398430402 (Hardback)
ISBN 9781398430426 (ePub e-book)
ISBN 9781398430419 (Audiobook)

www.austinmacauley.com

First Published 2022
Austin Macauley Publishers Ltd
1 Canada Square
Canary Wharf
London
E14 5AA

A big thank you to my amazing sister Yvonne for all the help and assistance.

And a huge thank you to everyone at Austin Macauley for all your hard work to get this book published.

And finally, a great thank you to the very talented illustrator Katharine Drees, for her wonderful illustrations.

When nine-year-old Andrew was told that he and his six-year-old sister, Gemma, would be going to stay at their grandparent's house again for a week or two during the summer, Andrew was ecstatic.

Because Andrew knew that staying at his grandparent's home meant eating plenty of pizza, hamburgers, plenty of ice cream and all the sweets he could eat.

It also meant having fun at the local park and enjoying Grandad's menagerie in his back garden. But what Andrew's grandad didn't tell Andrew about was a secret animal in his collection, a rather large one…

Chapter One

Andrew and Gemma Tyler were happy, in fact, they were very happy. The reason for this happiness: They were going to stay with their grandparents for a long weekend. They would do this several times a year, and as far as Andrew and Gemma were concerned, these weekends away were great holiday adventures; filled with fun and games, ice-cream, cakes and chocolate.

It was July, and the start of the summer holidays for the children. The weather was sunny and hot; and with no school, the kids just wanted to play and have fun.

Andrew and his sister were in Andrew's bedroom. Gemma was bouncing with joy on Andrew's bed, 'We're going to stay with Grandma and Grandad!' said Gemma over and over again.

'I can't wait,' said Andrew, 'I want to play in Grandad's garden again. I want to play hide and seek in his garden, yeah!'

The children started to run around Andrew's bedroom, jumping on his bed, as they did so, their mother called upstairs to them, 'Andrew, Gemma, make sure you pack your bags with everything you're going to need at Grandmother's house.'

'Okay, Mum,' Andrew and Gemma said together. Andrew was nine years old and his sister was six. Andrew picked up his large sports bag, which he used as a travel bag, and filled it with some clothes, his computer game console, and a picture book about spacecraft.

Gemma left Andrew's bedroom, walked into her bedroom, took out her pink travel case, which had a picture of a princess on it, from under her bed, and started to put what she would need into it.

As well as her clothes, Gemma made sure she brought along her favourite Teddy Bear, and her number one doll, her make-up bag, and her book about fairy-tales.

Soon the children were in their father's car with their mother, driving to the other side of town, on their way to their grandparent's house.

'Now, remember,' said their mother, 'be well-behaved for Nana and Grandad. Make sure you don't overexert them.'

'Nana and Grandad love having fun with us, mum,' said Andrew.

'And they always give us nice treats to eat,' added Gemma.

'Yes, but you heard your mother, kids, don't go too crazy around them; as they aren't as young as your mother and I,' said their father.

'Okay, Dad,' Andrew said. He was so looking forward to playing hide and seek in their house and back garden that he couldn't conceal his excitement.

'And make sure you both wash properly every morning, and if you play a lot in the back garden, make sure you shower or bathe afterwards, understand?' said their mother.

'Yes, mummy, we will,' said Gemma.

Before long, the Tyler family arrived at their grandparents' house. Nana opened the front door with a beaming smile, and Andrew and Gemma rushed up to her and hugged her.

As usual, when Andrew and Gemma went to stay with their grandparents, tea and lots of cakes would be waiting for them: strawberry cakes and chocolate cakes, vanilla cakes and banana cakes, ginger cakes and blueberry cakes.

Some cakes were bought from the local supermarket, but often Nana would bake these lovely cakes, especially for their grandkids; as baking cakes was one of Grandma's hobbies.

Like most children, Andrew scoffed down as much cake as he could eat. 'Don't eat too much at once, Andrew,' said his mother.

Grandma Joyce had a pet dog and cat, the dog was an old English sheepdog named Napoleon, and the cat was a moggy called Cleopatra. Gemma and Andrew loved these pets. Gemma liked to feed Napoleon cakes under the table, which the dog eagerly wolfed down.

Napoleon was such a big, soppy, old dog that Gemma would sometimes ride on his back around the living room.

As for their cat, Cleopatra, she had a look of indifference on her face, as all cats seem to have; no matter what was happening.

Andrew's grandparents had an open-plan living room/dining room, and while the children enjoyed their delicious cakes, Grandad asked Andrew's dad how his job was going.

'Same as usual, Alex,' said Andrew's dad. He was a manager at a factory in town, he worked in the shipping department, making sure the goods were sent out to customers.

While the adults were talking, the kids could hear squawks and hoots, and other animalistic sounds coming from the back garden: Grandad's Menagerie.

'Grandad, have you got any new animals in your Menagerie?' asked Andrew. Grandad often added new animals to his collection, usually when one of his animals died of old age, and had to be replaced with a new, young animal, sometimes a different species of animal.

'Well, young man,' said Grandad, 'as it happens, I do have a new addition or two.'

'Can we see them, Grandad?' asked Gemma, excitedly.

'Okay then, why not? I need to check on them anyway,' replied Grandad.

Gemma and Andrew looked at their mother, who nodded in agreement. Grandad opened the back doors that lead into the back garden, and the children rushed past him in a hurry. 'Yippee!' shouted Andrew.

'Yeah!' shouted Gemma.

'Play carefully,' said their father. While Grandad went to get the keys to the enclosures, the children ran around the garden, enjoying themselves; then they ran up to the fences of the enclosures and looked at the exotic animals that Grandad had in his collection.

Some of the animals in there, the children had already seen on previous visits to their grandparent's home, but there were one or two new additions. The animals that Grandad kept included: A big, bright Parrot with red, blue and yellow feathers, which the children knew was a Scarlet Macaw, who was called Captain Cook.

'Hello, Captain,' said Andrew to the colourful Parrot, and the Parrot squawked back in reply, as if understanding that Andrew had said hello to him. Gemma and Andrew both laughed at that.

'I see you're talking to old Captain Cook, again,' said their grandad, jangling his keys in his hands. 'Here Captain, I've got some little treats for you,' with that,

Grandad poked some large peanuts through the narrow gaps in the cage. The Parrot spread his colourful wings, and with a few flaps, flew over to the fence.

The Scarlet Macaw held on to the fence with his large clawed feet, and took the peanuts in his massive, hooked bill, and cracked open the shell of the peanut, easily; and then tossed the nut into his open bill.

The colourful Parrot squawked in what seemed like enjoyment, as he took more peanuts and swallowed them down his large bill.

Next door to the Scarlet Macaw's enclosure was the Monkey enclosure. This is where Grandad kept a small group of Marmoset Monkeys. These monkeys were small, funny-looking creatures, 'that one looks like a furry, little punk,' said Andrew.

'He does, doesn't he?' said Grandad, laughing. 'I could give you a haircut like that, if you want, Andrew,' said Grandad.

Gemma laughed and said, 'it would suit you so much.' The Marmoset Monkeys had lots of wooden climbing frames to climb inside their enclosure. 'Where are these monkeys from, Grandad, I mean, in the wild?' asked Gemma.

'This species comes from the Amazon Rainforest in Brazil, young Gemma,' said Grandad. Although these monkeys were raised in captivity, they're usually found in large, tropical rainforests.

The monkeys jumped about a lot and climbed up and down their wooden framed playground. 'Maybe I should put you two in there, hey,' said Grandad. 'You two are little monkeys sometimes.'

Gemma laughed, but Andrew looked a little bemused, then the children walked along to the next enclosure, which housed a female, Brazilian Tapir. The children's grandad poured some chopped-up vegetables into a tray at the bottom of the door to the Tapir's enclosure.

This mammal always amazed the kids, because she was quite large, dark brown in colour, with a snorkel-like nose. The Tapir had a deep pool in her enclosure for her to submerge and bathe in. 'This little beauty costs me a lot of money in food, but she's worth every penny,' chuckled Grandad. 'I raised her from a baby, when a local zoo didn't have any more room for another Tapir.'

'I love her big, strange nose,' said Gemma.

'Tapirs come from the Amazon too, little Gemma,' said Grandad.

'What do they eat in the wild?' asked Gemma, with keen interest.

'They eat a broad-range of vegetation.'

'So that makes them vegetarians, doesn't it, Grandad?' said Andrew.

'It does, but the word biologists use is a herbivore,' answered their grandad.

Does that mean they only eat herbs?' enquired Andrew.

Grandad laughed at this, 'they eat lots of different plants, young man.' Then Grandad suddenly remembered that he had to feed the young Black Caiman, which he kept in the enclosure next door.

'Hey, you two, do you want to watch me feed the little Crocodile that I have in the next enclosure?'

'Yes! Yes!' the children said, excitedly.

'Come on then,' said Grandad.

Grandad's enclosure occupied a large U shape at the bottom of the garden. Grandad and the kids walked from one side of the U shape to the other.

'You're gonna like this, kids,' said Grandad, and with that, Grandad took a bamboo stick, which he kept by the Caiman enclosure; he then opened a bucket, which contained cut-up bits of chicken.

Next, Grandad took a small piece of chicken and stuck it on the end of the bamboo stick. Then he stuck the stick through the fence and held it above the small pool of water.

Suddenly, the little Black Caiman leapt out of the water, and grabbed the piece of chicken with its mouth; then it pulled the meat down, under the water and disappeared in a large splash. 'Wow!' said Andrew. 'That was amazing.'

Grandad looked at the children seriously, and said, 'that thing would take your finger off, given half the chance.'

'How often do you feed the Caiman?' asked Gemma.

'Oh, I would say about once a week, young lady,' replied Grandad.

'Do you only feed it chicken, Grandad?' enquired Andrew.

'No, no, Andrew, I like to give it a variety of food, that way it keeps it more interesting, for the Caiman. In fact, if you're too naughty, I will feed you to the Croc, like Captain Hook and Peter Pan,' chuckled Grandad.

In the enclosure next to the Black Caiman, there lived a Great Grey Owl. The Owl was watching the family and the commotion going on in the Caiman pool; as the Caiman splashed about, trying to swallow the piece of chicken that Grandad had fed it.

'Your Great Grey Owl is amazing, Grandad,' said Gemma, 'he always sits there so still and silent.'

'Yes, he does, he's just watching and listening to everything,' said Grandad, yawning and stretching. 'I feed him mice that he swallows down whole. Did you know that when Owl's fly, they're as silent as the night?'

Just then, there was a short drumming sound, a short, deep rhythm, 'what was that, Grandad?' asked Andrew.

The children's grandad fumbled for an answer, for a second or two, then replied, 'Oh, oh, that was probably the Tapir, knocking against something in her enclosure,' said Grandad, quickly.

Changing the subject, he said, 'have you seen the Red River Hog, which I have lately? Let's go and see how he's getting on.'

'I didn't know Tapirs could make that sound, Grandad,' said Andrew.

'Neither did I,' chuckled Grandad. The family walked along to the next enclosure, which housed a Red River Hog, named Bruce. The children had seen him a number of times. He was one of their favourites.

'Are you going to feed Bruce the family leftovers, again, Grandad?' asked Gemma.

'Yes, I am, petal.' Replied Grandad; then he opened up a large plastic container, which contained food waste. Then Grandad took a plastic scoop and scooped up the food waste, then he dropped it through a hole in the door of the Red River Hog's enclosure.

'Go on boy, get your dinner,' said Grandad, then Grandad turned to Andrew, and said, 'do you remember where these animals come from in the wild?'

'South America,' answered Andrew, excitedly.

'No, they don't, young Andrew.'

'I know, Grandad,' interjected Gemma, 'they're from central and west Africa; you told us before.'

'Well remembered, little Gemma, they are, indeed, don't you love their Reddish colour?'

The Red River Hog rushed over to the food, always hungry and eager for a meal; his big snout moved up and down, like a big, organic suction hose, gobbling up the food.

'He'd eat me out of house and home, that big ol' boy,' said Grandad, 'but he's worth every penny, anything your grandma doesn't eat he munches down, so we don't waste anything in this house.'

The last animal in Grandad's collection was a beautiful Ocelot, a young female one. The children and their grandad walked up to the Ocelot's enclosure and peered through at the beautiful cat. The Ocelot was walking along a wooden beam, which Grandad had built himself; in fact, it was part of a whole network of wooden frames and beams, so the Ocelot could climb on and scratch at with its sharp claws. 'Isn't she a beauty?' said, Grandad.

'Yes, she is,' replied Andrew.

'What have you got in that enclosure, Grandad?' asked Gemma. She was pointing at an enclosure that looked a bit different to the rest. This was because the enclosure had a wooden board across the door, so it was hard to see inside.

Grandad had also put up a large, green tarpaulin all the way around the enclosure; once again, to make it difficult for anyone to look inside.

'Oh, in there—' Grandad stammered a bit '—in there, I just use for storage, you know, where I keep all the food for my animals. Let's go get some ice-cream,' said Grandad, hoping to distract the kids. 'I want Strawberry ice-cream, how about you two?'

'I want Chocolate ice-cream,' shouted Andrew.

'I want Vanilla ice-cream,' shouted Gemma. Then all three of them heard a deep huffing sound.

'What's that sound, Grandad?' asked Andrew, curiously.

'I don't know, lad, let's all have some ice-cream,' and with that, all three of them hurried back inside Grandad's house.

A few minutes later, Gemma, Andrew, Grandad and Grandma were all tucking into delicious bowls of ice-cream. 'This ice-cream is the best,' said Andrew, 'Grandma, can I go to my room and play my computer-game?'

'Yes, of course, you can,' replied Grandma.

'Can I go and get my fairy-tale book, and read it in the living room with you, Grandma?' asked Gemma.

'Sure you can, love,' said Grandma,

Sometime later, Andrew was in his bedroom, in his grandparent's home, playing his computer game, it was a game about a spaceship that had to fly over a distant planet, and fire at targets to earn points. Andrew loved being the pilot, it was great escapism for him, however, even space-pilots need a break from flying over distant planets. Andrew put his game-console down on his bed and walked over to the window.

His bedroom window overlooked the back garden, Andrew looked out at the big lawn and Grandad's Menagerie at the bottom of the garden.

Andrew looked at the mysterious enclosure, the one with the boarded-up entrance, and the green material around the fencing. He thought he could see a shape moving around the enclosure, a large, dark shape.

Andrew squinted his eyes, and looked once again, he wasn't sure if it was a trick of light and shadow; due to the sunlight filtering through the trees and down onto the fencing, or if there really was an animal inside the enclosure.

Just then, Andrew's grandad called to him, from downstairs, 'Andrew, that funny, practical-joke programme, is about to start on the TV. Do you want to watch it with us?'

'Yes, yes,' shouted Andrew, 'I'm on my way.'

It was night-time, about ten-thirty at night. Andrew's grandparents were sound asleep in their bed, Grandad could be heard snoring; happy and content, dreaming away in his own little world.

Moonlight shone through the gaps in the curtains, in Andrew's bedroom, and although his bedroom was quite dark, a light was visible under Andrew's duvet. It was coming from Andrew's torch: he was reading his book about Spacecraft.

Andrew wondered what it must be like to travel through space in a flying-saucer-like spaceship. He could imagine flying over distant planets and landing on them and then taking off again.

Andrew, would, of course, be the captain of the spaceship, and he would decide which planets to visit and for how long. Just then, Andrew heard a deep huffing sound coming from outside, the same sound he had heard earlier in the day.

'That's that sound again,' Andrew said to himself. Andrew switched his torch off, got out of bed, and without turning the lights on, pulled open the curtains, and looked out over the back garden.

Because there was a full moon, he could see the animal enclosures, but none of the animals inside. Andrew was so curious, he just had to know what was making that huffing noise. *Was there a secret animal in that mysterious enclosure? And if so, why had Grandad told him that there was nothing in there but stores of food for the animals?*

Andrew's body tingled with excitement, he loved games and adventure, and simply, curiosity had got the better of him; he had to go outside, into the back garden now, tonight. *Gemma,* Andrew thought, *I'll go and wake up Gemma, we can venture outside together.* After all, the back garden was dark, and a bit scary for Andrew at this time of night.

Andrew was wearing Pyjamas, he put his slippers on, he knew he had to be real quiet, as quiet as a mouse; or he would get caught, and be in real trouble with his Nan.

He walked softly to the bedroom door, turned the door handle slowly, and as gently as he could, opened the door, and stepped out onto the landing. Andrew stopped and listened, he could hear Grandad snoring away, but no other sounds. He crept along the landing towards Gemma's room, and turned the handle, it made a small noise, but not much; Andrew went inside and closed the door behind him.

'Gemma, Gemma,' Andrew whispered, 'are you awake?'

'Ah,' Gemma murmured, still half asleep, 'what is it?'

'I heard that noise again, from the back garden,' said Andrew.

'What noise?' asked Gemma.

'The sound, I mean the sound we heard this afternoon, from Grandad's enclosure; the one with that green fabric around it.'

'So, what do you want?' enquired Gemma, curiously.

'I want us to go and investigate what's making that sound,' Andrew said.

Gemma sat up in bed and looked puzzled at Andrew, 'But it's night-time, Andrew, we should be sleeping.'

'I know, I know, but I can't sleep when I'm curious; I want to know if there's an animal in that enclosure,' replied Andrew. 'We can sneak out the back door and have a quick look, while Grandad and Grandma are sleeping.'

'But Grandad has locked the back door,' said Gemma.

'Yes, but we know where the key for the back door is, it's on the key-hook, above the tea and coffee tins.'

'If our grandparents catch us outside, we're gonna be in big trouble,' said Gemma.

'But they won't catch us, because they're asleep, they don't have to know, we can have a quick look, then sneak back in again,' said Andrew.

Gemma thought about it for a few seconds, she nodded and said, 'Okay, let's do it.'

Gemma hopped out of bed, she was also wearing pyjamas, pink ones, and she put her slippers on and was ready to go out into the back garden.

Andrew said, 'Now remember, Gem, we have to be really quiet, otherwise we're going to wake up Grandad and Grandma, and we'll be in big trouble, you understand, don't you?'

'I do,' said Gemma, nervously.

'Okay, let's go, now stay behind me until we get outside,' said Andrew. Andrew walked over to Gemma's bedroom door, with Gemma close behind him, and turned the door handle, he then pulled the door open, quietly.

Andrew and Gemma both stood in the bedroom doorway just listening: the coast was clear. The children walked as quietly as they could towards the top of the staircase. Andrew looked at Gemma and put his index finger up to his lips, to indicate to Gemma, to be really quiet; then the kids began to creep down the stairs.

Halfway down the staircase, Andrew stopped to listen, luckily, their grandparents had not heard anything, so the kids continued going down. When they had got to the bottom of the staircase, Andrew suddenly remembered Grandma's dog, Napoleon; but fortunately, Napoleon was in his dog-basket, asleep in the living room, and the living room door was closed.

Andrew knew the cat, Cleopatra, would be asleep on the sofa, in the living room too, so he didn't have to worry about these pets waking their grandparents up.

Andrew and Gemma quietly walked along the hallway towards the kitchen, the door to the kitchen was open. Andrew saw the key to the back door, he reached up for it, over the kitchen counter, and quietly took the key.

Gemma looked at Andrew, her eyes opened wide, and she smiled and so did Andrew. Andrew turned around and crept towards the back door, he carefully and quietly, placed the key in the back door, and slowly turned the key. The door lock clicked open, Andrew turned the handle and opened the back door, but before stepping outside, he and Gemma stopped and listened again, for any signs of their grandparents, the house was silent.

'Come on,' Andrew whispered to his sister, and with that, they both stepped out into the big, dark garden. Andrew had his torch with him, Gemma moved closer to Andrew, as the dark garden was a bit scary for both of them; and Andrew turned his torch on.

A bright beam of white light shone in front of the kids, 'let's head towards the animal enclosures,' said Andrew, Gemma simply nodded in agreement.

Quietly, the children walked down the lawn, further and further away from the back door, both trying to be as quiet as they could be. After just a few seconds, the dark shapes of the animal enclosures became clearer.

Andrew shone his torch towards the left-side of the U shape enclosures, the white beam danced about until the children saw the brightly coloured parrot on his perch: 'Captain Cook.'

The parrot looked back at the children, but fortunately, didn't squawk.

Andrew shifted the torchlight along until it shone over the Marmoset Monkeys, being active mostly during the day, the monkeys were asleep. One or two began to stir, as the light of Andrew's torch was intrusive.

Andrew, realising this, kicked the torchlight off them, and along with Gemma, moved along to the next enclosure. The torchlight moved about, dashed left and right a bit, then fell upon the Tapir, lying on the floor of her enclosure, sleeping.

'We better not wake her up, Andrew,' said Gemma, quietly.

I agree,' Andrew replied, they walked further along, looking into the Caiman's enclosure. At first, the children couldn't see the Caiman, no matter where Andrew shone his torchlight. Then young Gemma noticed a pair of small eyes, in the middle of the pond in its enclosure, small, bright, motionless eyes. 'There it is,' said Gemma.

'Shhh,' said Andrew, in reply, 'we have to be quiet, remember?' His sister covered her mouth with her hands and nodded in agreement.

Moving along, the torchlight picked out the Great Grey Owl, perched high-up on a wooden frame; the owl just looked at Andrew and Gemma, like a guard-on-guard duty, somewhat stern, but silent.

Next, Andrew shone his torch into the Red River Hog enclosure, the large Red hog was sleeping. Then Gemma noticed something walking in the enclosure next to the

Red River Hog; it was the beautiful Ocelot, patrolling its enclosure.

Being a species of cat, the Ocelot was mainly nocturnal, and this Ocelot was wide awake. Andrew turned his torchlight onto the cat, its eyes glowed back like it was a creature from another world.

'Wow, its eyes are bright and shiny,' said Gemma.

'That's because cat's eyes reflect the light back,' Andrew said, 'I have read about it in a book at school.'

Suddenly, the Ocelot jumped up seven feet onto a wooden beam, the cat stretched its front legs and scratched at the wood; and then it walked along the beam like a Gymnast. Next, it jumped up onto a higher wooden beam and carried on walking around its enclosure on this aerial walkway.

Then suddenly, the children realised that they were next to the mysterious enclosure, the one with the board of wood nailed across the opening to the front door; the secret enclosure with green tarpaulin around it.

'Shall we look inside?' whispered Andrew to Gemma. His sister nodded yes, the kids crept closer to the front door of the cage, both very nervous at this moment, and not knowing what could possibly be in there.

Andrew, who was taller than his sister, hesitantly raised his torch and shone the light inside. Andrew stood on his tip-toes, to try and get a better view inside, the light of the torch danced around the enclosure fencing; Andrew thought he saw some movement, a black shape, large, but moving around.

'I think I saw something, Gemma,' said Andrew excitedly, Andrew refocused his efforts and shone the beam of light through the enclosure once again. A dark, hairy shape moved away from the light, which was flickering through the enclosure. 'There is something in here,' said Andrew, 'it's moving around, I can hear it too.'

Andrew had to get off his tip-toes for a few seconds, as it was getting uncomfortable. A deep huffing sound came from behind the door, 'see, did you hear that?' said Andrew.

'Yes, I heard it too,' said Gemma. Andrew gripped his torch firmly, once again, and then got back on to his tip-toes and shone the beam of light through the enclosure once again. Only this time, the light revealed a large face, it was the large face of a gorilla.

'Ahhh!' cried out Andrew, and he dropped his torch.

'It's a gorilla,' said Gemma, both children backed away from the enclosure.

The gorilla looked at them both, huffed and grunted, and stared at them some more. 'Wow,' said Andrew, 'it's a gorilla, Grandad's got a gorilla.'

Both Andrew and Gemma couldn't believe that there was a big gorilla in the enclosure. However, both children realised that time was passing by, and that they should go back indoors; after all, they had both had enough excitement for one night.

'We better go back into the house,' said Gemma, quietly to her brother.

'Yeah, I think you're right,' replied Andrew, still looking at the gorilla.

Chapter Two

'Andrew, Gemma, are you two up yet?' called Grandma Joyce, upstairs. 'Those two little scamps,' said Joyce to Grandad, 'I didn't know they liked their sleep so much.' Grandma Joyce carried on setting the table regardless.

Grandad Alex didn't seem to be bothered either way; he was reading the horse racing pages of one of the dailies. 'Think I'll put a few bets on today, there's a couple of Nags I like the look of in the three-fifteen at Kempston.'

'Please yourself,' replied Grandma Joyce, 'remember, I've got Rosemary and Cynthia coming over this afternoon, to bake cakes.'

'You little songbirds bake away, I'm staying out of it, and out of the kitchen when you're baking,' said Grandad, 'don't want to get under your feet, do I?'

Grandma Joyce placed a pot of fresh, hot, tea on the table, then looked up, 'Where are those two?' She walked out of the dining room, and over to the bottom of the staircase, she called upstairs again. 'Andrew and Gemma, come on, breakfast is ready.'

This time Andrew replied, 'Okay, Grandma, I'm coming down.'

'Be downstairs in a minute, Nanny,' called out Gemma from her bedroom. Andrew came out of his bedroom, still half asleep, he yawned and stretched his arms over his head, walked into the bathroom and began to splash water onto his face.

As Andrew dried his face with a towel, Gemma walked into the bathroom. 'Hey, Andrew, what about last night, wasn't that amazing?'

'Morning Gem, yeah, I still can't believe it, a gorilla in the garden.' Andrew suddenly looked a bit serious, 'but remember, we don't know anything about a gorilla, okay? Because we weren't supposed to be out that late at night, got it?'

'Yes, I understand,' said Gemma.

Before long the children were enjoying their breakfast of cereal; they both liked to have a mixture of cereals for breakfast: Crunchy Nut cornflakes and Fruit and Nut, they also drank tea that their Nan made them in copious amounts.

Grandad finished munching on a nice slice of toast, looked at the children, and then said, 'so, you two little munchkins, what are you doing today, got any plans?'

Andrew and Gemma both looked at each other quickly, then said together, 'we want to play in the back garden.'

'Do you now?' replied Grandad. 'Well, okay, that's fine with me and your nan, it's just I was driving into town, and wondered if you would like to go to the park?'

'Yes, yes, I want to go to the park, Grandad,' shouted Gemma.

'But what about our plans to play in the back garden, Gem?' said Andrew. Gemma suddenly remembered what Andrew really meant, but still wanted to play in the park; it was going to be a lovely, hot day and the ice-cream van would be there too.

'I know, Andrew, but the park is great fun, there are swings and slides, and we can ride our bicycles too.' Andrew realised, quickly, that his sister was right, of course, the park was too much like good fun to pass up.

'Yes, I want to go to the park, thanks, Grandad,' said Andrew.

Their grandad finished gulping down some tea, then said, 'Okay then, the park it is, but I have a few errands to do in town beforehand, okay?'

'Yes, Grandad,' said young Gemma, with a broad smile on her face.

Their grandma came into the dining room from the kitchen, she had heard the conversation, 'Okay my darling,' and kissed and hugged Gemma, 'you two go and get ready for the park, but behave properly for Grandad, and don't talk to any strangers.'

With that, the children hurried upstairs and got ready to go out.

After a while, the children and their grandad arrived at the local park. Their grandad had got a few things done in town, and was now looking forward to sitting on a park bench, and taking it easy.

Andrew and Gemma loved being in the park, and racing around on their bicycles; they liked to play 'Cops and Robbers,' this time, Andrew was the Cop, chasing around after, and always catching, Gemma the Robber. This was quite easy for Andrew, being nine years old and three years older than his sister.

Another game the kids liked to play, as their grandad looked on, was racing around the perimeter path of the park, doing laps. Andrew especially liked giving Gemma a head start, this was usually half a lap and doing his best to catch her up.

As Gemma raced around the park, she passed by her grandad, 'Go on Gem, you can do it, sweetheart,' shouted Grandad. Grandad laughed out loud at the determined look on the children's faces; taking it seriously.

Andrew lapped Gemma, 'See ya, sis,' he said, laughing as he flew past his sister. Andrew rode past his grandad, 'Grandad, Grandad, do you want to see me wheelie?'

'Sure, why not?' replied Grandad. Andrew slowed his bicycle down, steadied himself a bit, then lent backwards, and pulled on the handle-bars, his front wheel lifted off the ground a few inches, then a few inches more.

'Look, Grandad, look at me,' said Andrew.

'Very impressive, young man,' then Grandad chuckled to himself. Gemma, who was still riding around the park doing a lap, passed an elderly lady, who was sitting on a bench.

'Hello,' said Gemma to the elderly lady.

'Hello, my lovely, aren't you sweet?'

'Thank you,' said Gemma, 'do you like this park?'

The elderly lady replied, 'Yes, I do, it's lovely on a hot summer's day, isn't it?'

'Yes, it is. My brother and I are racing each other,' said Gemma.

'Yes, I've been watching you two, riding around, enjoying yourselves; do you want me to show you some magic?' said the elderly lady.

'What's magic?' enquired Gemma.

'Well, you close your eyes and count to ten, and I'll show you magic when you open them,' said the elderly lady.

'Okay then,' said Gemma, 'one, two, three, four, five, six, seven, eight, nine, and ten.' Then Gemma opened her eyes and was amazed to see five balloons attached to the back of her bicycle; a red one, a blue one, a green one, a yellow one, and a white balloon. 'Wow, that's amazing,' Gemma said, still not really believing how the balloons got there, 'how did you do that?'

'Like I said, it's magic, darling, magic,' replied the elderly lady. By now, Andrew had noticed the balloons on Gemma's bicycle, he raced over to his sister and the mysterious lady.

'Where did you get the balloons from, Gem?' asked Andrew.

'This kind woman gave them to me, by magic,' answered his sister.

'Can I have some balloons for my bike, please?' said Andrew to the elderly lady.

'Of course, you can,' she said, 'just close your eyes and wish real soon, that one day you'll fly to the moon.' Andrew closed his eyes and covered them with his hands too, he made the wish that the elderly lady suggested and then opened his eyes. And sure enough, Andrew's bicycle had the same colourful balloons attached to it as his sister's had.

'Wowee!' shouted Andrew, 'how did you do it? I mean, that's incredible.'

The elderly lady laughed, 'there's nothing to it, my dear.' Just then, everyone heard the unmistakable chimes of an ice-cream van arriving at one side of the park.

'Gem, Gem, let's ask Grandad for an ice cream, quick,' said Andrew. The kids got back onto their bicycles, said goodbye and thanked the mysterious elderly lady for the balloons.

'Bye, bye, my dears, you never know, we may meet again, one day,' said the lady. And then Andrew and his sister raced as fast as they could, over to where their grandad was sitting.

The children's grandad was beginning to doze off in the lovely, warm, summer sunshine. 'Grandad, grandad,' shouted Andrew, this jolted their grandad awake.

'Ah, who, what?' mumbled Grandad.

'Can we have an ice cream, please, Grandad?' said Gemma.

'Yes, of course, you can my little petal,' replied Grandad. Then their grandad noticed where the ice-cream van was, and all three of them started to make their way across the park.

Then Grandad noticed the balloons on the children's bikes, 'where did you get those balloons from?' asked their grandad.

'A kind elderly lady gave them to us. She did it by magic,' said young Gemma.

'Did she really?' said Grandad, a bit surprised. After a minute or so, they had reached the ice-cream van. 'So, my little Munchkins, what flavour of ice-cream do you want then?' enquired Grandad.

'I want chocolate with that raspberry ripple sauce on it,' shouted Andrew.

'I want a Ninety-Nine, Grandad, with a chocolate flake in it, and raspberry sauce, please,' said Gemma.

'Alright then,' said Grandad, the ice-cream man had heard them clearly, so he started making their ice-creams. 'And I'll have a Ninety-Nine too, with the raspberry sauce but no flakes, please,' said Grandad, to the ice-cream man.

'Right you are, boss,' said the ice-cream seller. He was a short, chubby man with a moustache, which kind of made him look like a villain in a children's movie.

'That comes to seven pounds fifty, please, boss,' said the ice-cream man. Grandad paid the man, got his change, and then they all went back inside the park. As the three of them walked through the park, Andrew and Gemma pushing their bikes with one hand, and licking their ice-creams with the other, their grandad said, 'this ice-cream is so delicious.'

'So is this one,' said Gemma, with vanilla ice-cream on her face.

'My ice-cream is yummylicious, it's the best ice-cream there is,' said Andrew, as though he was in some sort of ice-cream heaven. After walking a little while, Grandad and the kids came to the swings and the slides; by now, they had just about finished their ice-creams, and were eager to play.

Gemma made her way over to the slides, she didn't even ask her grandad if it was okay to go on them or not. Andrew made his way to the Swings, 'now you two be careful on those things, hold on tight and watch what you're doing,' said Grandad, a bit sternly for emphasis.

Gemma got to the top of the slide, shouted 'yeahhhh!' As she slid down with her arms raised over her head. Their grandad smiled at them having fun, he remembered being young and playing on swings and slides, many years before – happiness.

As Andrew swung on his swing, he called over to his grandad, 'Grandad, can you take us to the sweet shop today?'

Their grandad laughed, 'sweets as well as ice-cream,' he let the children wonder for a second or two, and then answered, 'you bet I can, seeing how you two have been so good for me, but don't tell your parents, 'cause I'm not supposed to buy you too many sweets.'

'Thank you, Grandad!' shouted out Andrew and Gemma together. Just then, Grandad suddenly remembered the horse race that he bet on, he needed to know which horse had won. These days even grandparents have mobile phones, Grandad took out his mobile and got on to the internet, and typed in the race he was interested in. A list of the horses and where they finished popped up on the screen.

Grandad's horse was called General Washington, unfortunately for Grandad, his horse came third. 'You win some, you lose some,' said Grandad to himself.

The shadows of the trees in the park began to lengthen, and so, in due course, Andrew, Gemma and their grandad, made their way to the sweet shop that the children liked to go to.

Inside the sweet shop, children and their parents looked at a multitude of sweets; the woman who worked behind the counter had a nice disposition, very kind and welcoming. 'Hello,' she said to Andrew and Gemma, 'what can I get you?'

'I would like some chocolate buttons and those strawberry and lemon sweets, please, half and half,' said young Gemma, to the woman behind the counter.

'Certainly,' the woman said, 'would you like a small, medium, or large bag?'

Gemma looked at her grandad, then at the woman, then back at her grandad. 'Okay then, make it a large bag,' said Grandad to the sweet shop woman. While the woman was taking down the plastic jars that contained the sweets that Gemma wanted, Grandad asked Andrew what sweets he would like.

'I want a large bag of Jellybeans, please, Grandad.'

'Right you are, then, my little piglet,' replied Grandad.

'Jellybeans, large bag?' said the woman behind the counter, just to confirm that she had heard them correctly.

'That's right, please,' said Grandad. As the woman scooped Jellybeans into a paper bag, Andrew whispered to Gemma, 'and you know who they are really for, don't you?'

His sister suddenly realised who Andrew meant, 'are they?' Gemma asked Andrew.

'Yes, tonight, but you know, shush,' and with that, Andrew placed his index finger against his lips.

Chapter Three

While Andrew, Gemma and their grandad were at the park, having fun, Grandma Joyce had a visit from two of her close friends: Cynthia and Rosemary; these ladies were about the same age as Grandma Joyce.

Cynthia was wearing a nice purple dress with a flowery pattern on it, with a purple ladies' hat to match, and nice leather black shoes. Rosemary was wearing a light blue dress, with thin, black stripes running through it, and white shoes, which were probably leather.

Both ladies, Cynthia and Rosemary were a little round in figure, as was Grandma Joyce; you might say, they were all a little overweight. Partly, because they did like to eat cake, especially cakes they baked themselves.

The three ladies had all just finished having some tea and cake, that Grandma Joyce had given them all, then Joyce said, 'well, ladies shall we do some baking then?'

'Yes, let's,' replied Rosemary, and the ladies cleared away their cups and plates, and started to put ingredients for baking cakes on the table. The ingredients they would use were as follows:

Sugar
Eggs
Self-rising flour
Milk
Chocolate

Raisins
Butter
Mixed dried fruit
Ginger
Glazed
Cherries
Apricots
Marzipan
Blueberries
Raspberries

Then the three 'Chefs' each placed a mixing bowl on the kitchen table and then started to put their ingredients into the mixing bowls. Grandma Joyce turned on the oven, it was a large oven as she liked cooking, especially baking, large enough to fit three cake tins in it.

Grandma Joyce said, 'shall I turn the radio on ladies, shall we have a little music while we bake?'

'Yes, we usually do, don't we?' replied Cynthia. A song with a good upbeat tempo was playing on the station that Grandma's radio was tuned to. So, in-between mixing their cake mix, the three ladies would have a little dance around the kitchen table; and beat their mixing spoons to the rhythm of the music.

Little puffs of baking flour would shoot up into the air, every time one of the ladies struck their mixing bowl, or the kitchen table.

Joyce started to spin around, laughing to herself, as she did so, 'you could use those moves at next month's Church dance, Joyce,' said Cynthia, chuckling as she spoke.

Rosemary mixed her cake mix, 'you know ladies, one of us will probably win the baking competition tomorrow afternoon,' she said.

'Well Joyce, your delicious fruit cake won it last month,' said Cynthia.

'Wasn't that cake lovely with a cup of tea,' said Rosemary.

'Thank you, my dears, it's very nice of you to say so,' said Grandma Joyce. 'After all, the main thing is having cakes that we can sell by the slice, to raise money for the church's good causes,' continued Joyce.

'And what better way to raise money for the church, than having tea and cake afternoons,' said Rosemary.

After a short while, the three ladies had finished mixing their cake mix and they each began to pour their mix into their baking tins. As they did so, Cynthia said, 'are your grandkids staying with you, Joyce?'

'Yes, they are,' replied Joyce.

'It must be so lovely to have them around,' said Rosemary.

'Oh, they do keep me and Alex young, that's for sure, little Gemma's good as gold, and Andrew's well behaved enough; for a little boy,' said Grandma Joyce.

'I bet they're running rings around your husband, right now, Joyce,' said Cynthia.

'Oh, that big 'ol kid, he loves it,' said Joyce. 'And it does him good to get out of the house, get him off that sofa and out from under our feet, while we bake,' said Joyce. All three of the women started laughing at that.

Grandma Joyce made everyone a large pot of tea, and after a short time had passed, their cakes were ready. Delicious smells filled the kitchen and indeed, the whole of the downstairs; a blend of fruit cake and chocolate, marzipan and ginger, the house smelled like a bakery.

Grandma Joyce opened the oven door, she had her oven-gloves on, and so took out each cake, one by one, 'here we are then, it looks like they all came out well,' she said.

'Well, everyone at the church should love these cakes,' said Rosemary. Then the women heard a key opening the front door, Grandad and the Grandkids were back.

Andrew and Gemma rushed into the house, happy and excited, 'hello, Grandma,' said Gemma.

'Hello, my sweetheart, did you have a good time at the park?'

'Yes, we had a great time,' said Gemma.

'We had delicious ice-cream in the park,' said Andrew.

'Lucky you,' said Grandma Joyce, 'Rosemary, Cynthia and I have just finished Baking.'

Grandad walked into the kitchen, 'hi, love, I'm bushed, those kids have worn me out,' he said.

'Would you like a nice cup of tea?'

'Oh, yeah, that would be great, pet,' said Grandad.

'Right, I'll make you all a nice cup of tea,' said Grandma Joyce.

While their grandparents were in the kitchen, Andrew and Gemma sat in the living room, watching TV.

'Andrew,' said Gemma.

'Yeah,' replied Andrew, watching the TV screen.

'Are we gonna sneak out again, and visit the gorilla later?' Andrew turned to Gemma. 'Yes, we are, but keep it down, it's a secret mission, no adults must know; I'm going to give him some jellybeans.'

Gemma nodded her head, 'okay, but what time are we going to go outside?'

'We'll go outside at midnight,' said Andrew.

Chapter Four

It was midnight, the house was quiet, and Andrew was ready to go outside. Andrew had his jeans, sweatshirt and white trainers on; ready for the back garden.

He had already pulled the curtains in his bedroom and was looking at the enclosures at the bottom of the garden. Andrew could make out the shapes of the enclosures, but they were vague and fuzzy from this distance, almost as one would see them in a dream.

Andrew turned around and quietly walked across his bedroom, he opened his bedroom door, as silently as he could, and listened. Then Andrew stepped out of his bedroom, closed his door quietly, and crept along the landing to his sister's bedroom.

Andrew opened Gemma's door, and in the semi-darkness, could see his sister standing there, dressed and ready too.

'Hi, Gem,' Andrew whispered, 'are you ready to go outside?' Gemma nodded in agreement, and they both left Gemma's bedroom, listening as they moved. The children both adopted a slow-motion walk as they made their way towards the staircase.

Slowly, the kids moved down the staircase, careful not to make a sound, although this was virtually impossible; they did make a very small amount of noise as they stepped, but while their grandparents slept they could not be heard, or could they?

Suddenly, Andrew and Gemma heard the unmistakable sound of feet walking around their grandparent's bedroom, they had been heard. The footsteps moved across the room, they heard the bedroom door open, Andrew and Gemma froze, hearts in their mouths; at any moment they expected to hear one of their grandparents telling them off, for being up this late.

The landing light went on, the kids could tell by the movement of the person, that it was their grandmother. Then Andrew and Gemma heard the Bathroom door open: Grandma had to spend a penny.

While their grandma was in the bathroom, Andrew told Gemma to squat down on the stairs, they both did this; to reduce the chance of being seen by their gran, when she came out of the bathroom.

The children heard the lavatory flush, then the tap of the basin running, a few seconds later, the bathroom door opened and the kids heard their nan walk back into her bedroom, turning the landing light off as she went.

Gemma and her brother sighed a big sigh of relief; it was a close call, but their adventure could continue. Being as quiet as he could, Andrew lifted the back door key of the key holder, brought it to the back door and placed it in the key-hole, turned the key quietly, the door unlocked.

Andrew and Gemma paused for a moment to listen, when they thought it was safe to continue, they opened the back door, and softly closed it behind them.

Walking down the lawn, Andrew and Gemma giggled to each other in childish excitement. Andrew reached into his pocket, and pulled out a packet of jellybeans, 'do you think he'll like them?' said Andrew to his sister.

'I don't know, I hope so, and how do you know it's a boy?' said Gemma.

'Not sure, I just get a feeling that it's a male gorilla,' replied Andrew.

A few seconds later the children had reached the animal enclosures. Andrew looking up at the door opening to the enclosure, made a pssst sound with his mouth. Nothing. After a few seconds, Andrew tried again, making the same sound. But the gorilla did not appear at the opening in the door.

Gemma and Andrew looked at each other, a little bemused, *where was the gorilla? Why didn't he appear?* 'He's not there,' said Andrew wondering what to do next, as he did so, he started to eat the jellybeans he had in his hands.

'Let's have some, Andrew,' said Gemma, Andrew offered the bag to his sister, Gemma started chewing away, and they tasted and smelled delicious.

Andrew was chewing his jellybeans, when suddenly, the gorilla appeared at the door opening, Andrew got a start, dropped his packet of jellybeans, with a gasp.

Gemma said, 'oh!'

The big gorilla just stared at the kids, didn't make a sound, he seemed to be checking the children out. Andrew, not knowing what else to do at that moment, picked up the packet of jellybeans, and slowly brought the sweets over to the big gorilla, scared, but excited too.

'Hello,' said Andrew to the big gorilla, the gorilla looked at Andrew, as though the gorilla was wondering what Andrew was. 'We came along to visit you,' said Andrew to the ape.

'The jellybeans, Andrew, offer him a jellybean,' said Gemma.

"Oh, yeah, you're right, Gem,' Andrew replied, remembering now why he had brought the jellybeans, in the first place.

Andrew lifted the packet of jellybeans up to the great gorilla's face, Andrew's hand was shaking, somewhat, but that was understandable. Andrew brought the packet just under the gorilla's nose; the gorilla sniffed them.

'You eat them, you see, they're really delicious,' said Andrew to the big ape, hoping he could understand, somehow. 'Look, like this,' said Andrew, he then put his other hand into the packet, and took out several jellybeans, and started eating them. 'They're very chewy,' mumbled Andrew, with his mouth full of sweets.

Just then, Gemma put her hand into the packet of jellybeans and ate some, chewing away with delight. The big gorilla made a low, deep sound from his mouth, as though he was enquiring about the jellybeans.

Andrew took out some more jellybeans and brought them over to the gorilla's large head; the gorilla sniffed these too, then the big ape reached out with his large hand, to take some of the sweets.

Andrew and his sister couldn't believe it, Andrew placed the sweets into the gorilla's padded hand, and then the ape ate them. The gorilla chewed the sweets like Andrew and Gemma did; then he started to make excited, huffing noises, like he was enjoying himself.

'Yeah!' shouted Gemma. 'He likes them.' Then the gorilla opened the palm of his big hand, to indicate that he wanted more jellybeans, this made Andrew really excited.

'I don't believe it, Gem, he wants more jellybeans,' said
Andrew. As Andrew brought the packet of sweets closer to the gorilla's hand, the big ape started to make short,

huffing sounds, like he was getting excited too. Andrew poured more jellybeans into the gorilla's hand, and the gorilla quickly put the sweets in his mouth and started chewing them.

Then Gemma noticed something, 'look, Andrew, what's that around his neck?'

'What's what?' replied Andrew, a bit confused.

'There's something around his neck, it's small and shiny,' said Gemma.

'Yes, you're right, Gem, but it's hard to see in this dark, light; I know, I'll use my torch,' said Andrew.

Andrew took out his torch, which he had in his back pocket, and turned it on. Andrew didn't want to shine the bright light in the gorilla's face, like before; he didn't want to scare him. So, he raised the torchlight up, very slowly, and then, as carefully as he could, shone the torchlight onto the chest of the great ape.

Andrew then raised the beam of the light up, just a little more, and saw that the small, metallic, object was a name-tag. 'Gemma, Gemma,' said Andrew, 'it's a name-tag.'

'What is his name?' asked Gemma.

Andrew looked a little closer, to be certain, 'his name is Fudge,' answered Andrew.

'Fudge?' said Gemma. 'That's a great name.'

'Here, Fudge,' said Andrew, 'it's only right with a name like Fudge, that you have some more sweets.' And with that, Andrew poured the last of the jellybeans, into the open hand of the gorilla.

The ape shovelled the sweets into his mouth, straight away, then stretched his hand through the bars of his enclosure, to ask for more.

'I'm sorry, Fudge, I don't have any more sweets left to give you, but I'll get you lots more, I promise.' Andrew reached out his hand to touch the gorilla's, Andrew's hand looked small next to the big gorilla's hand, a few seconds later, their fingertips touched each other, and a magical connection happened.

'We better head back indoors now, Andrew,' said Gemma, aware that time was passing by.

'Okay,' replied Andrew, he was still looking at the big gorilla, amazed by this incredible animal. 'We'll come and visit you tomorrow night,' said Andrew to Fudge, the big gorilla. The gorilla made a few deep huffing sounds, almost as if he was talking back to Andrew.

As Gemma and her brother walked back across the lawn to the house, they both tingled with excitement; they now actually had a gorilla as a playmate.

Chapter Five

The next morning was sunny, sunlight shone brightly through the living room of Andrew's grandparent's home, Andrew and Gemma were sat on the sofa, watching cartoons on TV. The children laughed out loud, as Roadrunner got the better of Coyote.

The children's grandmother was reading her morning newspaper, and drinking tea, then she said to Andrew and Gemma, 'we're going to the supermarket in town, this morning, and you two have to come with us.'

'Okay, Grandma,' said Gemma, still looking at the TV screen.

'When are we leaving, Grandma?' said Andrew.

'Well, your grandad is in the shower, at the moment, and he's already had his breakfast; so in about fifteen minutes, I should imagine,' replied their grandmother.

'Good,' said Andrew, 'we can watch more cartoons.'

Sometime later, Gemma, Andrew and their grandparents were strolling around Sainsbury's, it was a large supermarket, with many aisles. Their grandmother wanted to look at some clothes, so she left her husband with the Grandkids for a few minutes.

Andrew saw this as an opportunity, 'Grandad,' he said, 'can you push me and Gemma in the trolley, while it's quiet?'

'Oh, go on, then,' said Grandad, 'get in, you little monkeys.' Andrew climbed up onto the trolley, first, then he helped his sister get in.

'Push us, Grandad, we want to go fast,' said Gemma.

'I don't know how fast I can push you,' said Grandad. Grandad gave a push, and the trolley rolled forward, gaining speed, as it went down the aisle.

'Yeah!' shouted Andrew. 'This is great fun.' Andrew and his sister were sitting near the front of the trolley, so their grandad lent over the back of the trolley, and lifted his feet off the ground.

'I haven't done this in a long time,' said Grandad. Then the kid's grandad saw that the aisle was going to end at a junction with another aisle, he thought it was a good time to apply the 'brake,' so he lowered his feet back down onto the floor, and used the heels on his shoes to slow the trolley down.

Just then, the children's grandma came back over to them, 'You're worse than they are,' she said to their grandad; 'I was watching you from over there.'

'Well, we're only having a bit of fun, love,' said Grandad, 'at my age, I'll take any fun I can get,' and then Grandad started laughing.

'Don't you two encourage him,' said their grandma, 'he's bad enough as it is,' said Grandma to the kids.

'Anyhow, I haven't finished looking at the dresses they have, over there,' said Grandma, looking at Grandad, 'you better get on and do the food shopping, while I look at the clothes.'

'Right, you are, pet,' said Grandad, affectionately, 'we're gonna get on with that, then, see you in a bit.' Grandad took hold of the trolley, and started to head towards the Fruit and Veg section; after all, there was a lot of fruit and veg to get for his animals.

Andrew and Gemma tagged along with their grandad, then Gemma said, 'Grandad, can we have some jellybeans, please?'

'Jellybeans? Didn't I buy you a packet of jellybeans yesterday?'

'Yes, you did,' replied Gemma, 'but can you buy us some more, please?'

'Oh, I'm not sure, my lovely, after all, your mother told me not to give you too many sweets.'

'Please, Grandad,' said Andrew, 'we really love jellybeans.'

'Well, I'll tell you what,' said Grandad, 'I'll buy you both a small packet of jellybeans each; and I'm gonna buy a big chocolate cake, a really big one, so the family can have some, and some of my animals too.'

'Thanks, Grandad,' said Andrew and Gemma at the same time.

'Now, it's most important that I buy some bananas,' said their grandad; 'a lot of the animals love 'um.'

'Who likes them the most, Grandad?' asked Andrew, trying to get some information out of his grandad.

For a second, grandad was caught off-guard, a bit, and he said, 'oh, that big ole hairy boy of mine.'

'Big old hairy boy?' enquired Gemma.

'Oh, I mean, er, I mean,' Grandad fumbled his words for a second or two, 'I mean Old Bruce, you know, Big Bruce the Red River Hog.'

'Oh, Bruce,' said Gemma, 'yes, we know.'

At the Fruit and Veg section, Grandad placed lettuces and carrots and parsnips into the trolley, 'do you know who these are for?' asked Grandad to Gemma and Andrew, the kids thought about it for a minute, then said, 'the parrot?'

'No, not the parrot, old Captain Cook gets nuts and fruit,' said Grandad, 'the vegetables are for big boy Bruce, the Red River Hog.'

'And bananas,' shouted Gemma.

'Yes, and bananas too,' said Grandad, 'the Tapir will eat lettuces and other veg,' continued their grandad. 'Now, I need lots of fruit, I'm gonna need bananas, apples, oranges, pears and maybe a few other fruits,' said Grandad.

'For the Red River Hog and Tapir,' said Andrew.

'And the Marmoset Monkeys and the parrot likes fruit too,' replied their grandad.

'What kind of nuts do you need, Grandad?' asked Andrew, curiously.

'I feed him a mixture of nuts, always have, and a good mixture of fruit; I think that's best for him, a better selection of tastes for the captain,' said Grandad.

'Do you ever feed the Crocodile nuts, Grandad?' asked Gemma.

'You mean the Caiman, oh, no, he can't eat nuts or fruit and veg; no that thing needs to eat meat; it's a carnivore.'

'That means it eats meat,' said Andrew.

'Yes, I feed it chicken breast cuts, and mice,' answered Grandad.

'Mice?' said Gemma, quizzically, 'where do you get mice from, Grandad?'

'Well, I get mice from a company that the man at the pet shop told me about,' said Grandad. 'They send me dead ones and live ones to feed to my Owl, Caiman and Ocelot.'

Andrew's grandad looked at Andrew, and said, 'and I can always feed little boys that misbehaviour to them too.' Their grandad laughed out loud, 'only teasing you, lad.'

'The animals are really lucky that you buy all this food for them, aren't they, Grandad?' said Gemma.

'Yes, they are, my little cherry pie, as you can see, there's a hell of a lot of work that goes into keeping animals,' stated Grandad. 'Still, it's one of my hobbies, and I do enjoy keeping them all.'

The family then made their way over to the Cake section of the supermarket, and as promised, Grandad bought a large, chocolate cake.

Back at their grandparent's home, Andrew and Gemma went out to play in the back garden. Andrew wanted to play football, and he talked Gemma into playing too. The children also ate their jellybeans while they played football; the kids couldn't help looking over at Grandad's Menagerie, and especially at the enclosure where they knew the big gorilla was.

Andrew made a goal out of a pair of old trainers, and stuck his sister in it, as the goalie. Andrew thought he was quite good at football, and liked to shoot from distance. When Andrew scored a goal, he would celebrate like he was a Premier Footballer, running around the garden, with his arms up in the air.

The children didn't play at that fast a pace, so they continued to eat and chew their jellybeans with delight. Gemma liked saving shots from Andrew, when she could; every time she would save a shot, she shouted, 'Yeah!'

Then Andrew suddenly realised that he had eaten all his jellybeans. 'Hey, Gem, I've eaten all my jellybeans, how about you?'

'I've still got a few left, but only a few,' said Gemma, then Gemma remembered that they were supposed to save some jellybeans for 'Fudge,' the gorilla. 'How are we going to get the gorilla to play with us, without sweets?' asked Gemma.

Andrew thought about it for a few seconds, then said, 'no it's okay, because we can bring the gorilla a big slice of chocolate cake, from the cake that's in the fridge.'

'There's also something else I want to do tonight,' said Andrew to his sister.

'What's that?' asked Gemma.

'I want to bring 'Fudge' out of his enclosure.'

'We can't do that,' said Gemma, worryingly.

'Why can't we? We know where Grandad keeps the keys to the animal enclosures; they're kept next to the back door key.' Andrew looked around, to make sure Nan or Grandad weren't within hearing range, then he continued; 'we take all the keys, they're on the same key ring, anyway, and we unlock 'Fudges' door, then he can play with us in the back garden.'

'Wow,' said Gemma, 'are we really going to let the gorilla out?'

'Yes, we are,' said Andrew, 'the gorilla likes us, I'm sure he does; we gave him jellybeans to eat, remember? Once we give him a big slice of chocolate cake, he'll like us even more,' said Andrew, looking to convince his sister.

'But remember, Gem, it's another secret mission, only for us kids to know, no adults must find out, got it?'

'Yes, yes,' said Gemma, nodding her head in agreement.

Chapter Six

Midnight arrived again, Andrew and Gemma were ready once again. The brother and sister were getting used to being up and dressed at midnight; they were both getting the hang of opening their bedroom doors quietly. Both of them got better at walking on the upstairs carpet and staircase, without making that much noise.

It also helped the children's 'mission' that both their grandparents were deep-sleepers. Andrew and his sister reached the kitchen, Andrew softly opened the fridge door, listening all the while for any signs that his grandparents might be up.

The house was quiet and Andrew continued, he looked inside the fridge, saw the large, white cake-box and removed it from the fridge, and opened it. Even though the kitchen was in darkness, some light from the outside shone through the window.

Andrew looked at the big, brown, chocolate cake, he then placed it on the kitchen table. Next, Andrew took a plate and a butter knife, and then cut a large slice of chocolate cake and placed it on the plate.

'Right, now we need the keys,' said Andrew, quietly, to young Gemma. Andrew took the keys for the back door and all the keys to the animal enclosures.

'Gemma, you carry the plate with the cake, and I'll unlock the back door,' said Andrew. Andrew put the key in the back door, just like on the other nights, and turned the key, quietly; then the kids opened the door and went outside.

There was a quarter moon in the sky, so there was plenty of light for the children to see things in the back garden. Soon Andrew and his sister were at the gorilla enclosure. Gemma said, 'but which key unlocks the door?' Whilst holding the plate with the big, chocolate cake on it.

'I don't know, I'm just gonna have to try them all until I find the right one,' answered Andrew. There were eight keys on the key ring, one for each enclosure. Andrew tried the first key, but the door did not unlock.

Andrew tried the second key, but that was not the right one, either. He tried again, but no luck, then Andrew tried the fourth key on the key ring; this key fitted the lock, 'it's this one, Gemma,' said Andrew, unable to contain his excitement.

'Gemma, you put the plate down in front of the door, so big Fudge can see the chocolate cake,' said Andrew. Then Andrew turned the key in the lock and opened the door to the gorilla enclosure.

The children looked into the dark doorway, but saw nothing, they didn't hear anything, either. A few seconds passed, which seemed like minutes, to Andrew and Gemma. Then out of the darkness, a large, dark shape emerged, big and powerful, a huge male gorilla stood in the doorway.

The large gorilla at first, had a rather serious look on his face, this scared the children. Andrew was beginning to think that letting the gorilla out was not such a good idea, after all.

The big ape sniffed the air, then looked down and saw the chocolate cake on the plate, the gorilla's face changed, his eyes opened wide, and he seemed to smile.

Next 'Fudge' moved out of his enclosure, by lifting himself up, on to all fours, and knuckle-walked up to the plate, and the chocolate cake. The gorilla looked at Andrew and Gemma, made two huffing sounds, deep and short, then picked up the chocolate cake and started eating it.

It was obvious the big gorilla loved the chocolate cake, he had chocolate all around his mouth, he made several, deep, huffing sounds, again, then scoffed the rest of it.

The kids were so happy that 'Fudge' liked the chocolate cake that they had brought him, Andrew said, 'hello Fudge, we came to see you again, we're glad you like the cake.'

The large ape looked at Andrew, it seemed like he understood what Andrew had said to him. Then big Fudge looked at Gemma, she smiled back, Gemma was in awe of the huge size of the gorilla.

Then Fudge waved his arms a little, beckoning the children nearer, Andrew and Gemma glanced at each other, then they approached the large ape. The kids were not afraid at all; they could sense that big Fudge was a gentle giant.

Then the big gorilla placed his left arm around Andrew and his right arm around Gemma, and he hugged them. This made the children very happy indeed, and Gemma cried out, 'YEAH!'

Next, big Fudge looked like he wanted to play, he started to get excited, he moved his body up and down, whilst being on all fours, made some deep, huffing and grunting noises, and then took off around the garden.

The gorilla ran in a large circle around the lawn, huffing as he went, it seemed he loved being out of his restrictive enclosure.

'Yeah! Yeah! Yeah!' shouted Andrew. 'Go on Fudge!'

'He loves playing, Andrew,' said young Gemma. Luckily for Andrew and Gemma, their grandparent's bedroom was at the front of the house, overlooking the front garden, so they were further away from the back garden, and the commotion going on there.

The gorilla ran round and round the garden, making deep huffing noises as he moved, the ape looked at Andrew and nodded his head up and down.

Then he slowed down and stopped, he looked at the children, then he waved them over with his huge hand. The kids walked up to big Fudge, then the huge gorilla picked up Andrew with his large, left hand and placed him on his back; then he picked up Gemma with his right hand, and placed her on his back, directly behind her brother.

Then the gorilla made deeper, huffing and grunting noises, it was as though the big ape was trying to tell them something. Andrew and his sister held on to the gorilla by grasping his thick, black hair, then Fudge started moving around the garden again.

The gorilla ran faster and faster around the lawn, with Andrew and Gemma holding on tightly. 'This is great fun!' shouted Andrew to Gemma.

'I love it!' shouted back Gemma. Round and round the garden they ran, and up and down the length of the lawn, big Fudge had boundless energy.

'Keep holding on tight, Gemma,' said Andrew, 'I don't want you to fall off.'

'I am holding on tightly, Andrew,' shouted back Gemma. Then Fudge slowed down and came to a stop in one corner of the garden. The gorilla had noticed something – a wheelbarrow. The ape approached the wheelbarrow, clearly not sure what it was, he sniffed it, then touched it, huffing deep sounds as he did so.

Then the gorilla picked up Andrew and Gemma once again, and placed them in the wheelbarrow. 'I think he wants to push us along,' said Andrew to his sister. Then Fudge placed his large hands on the handles of the wheelbarrow, and lifted it up, and started to push it.

The big gorilla made more huffing and grunting sounds, as he pushed the children faster and faster. 'Yeah!' shouted Gemma, 'this is like being on a ride at a theme park.'

'This is great fun!' shouted Andrew. 'Fudge likes to play as much as we do.' Fudge pushed the wheelbarrow around the garden several times, at quite some speed; then, as if knowing exactly what to do, the large ape brought the wheelbarrow to a stop, and back at the same place he had found it.

The children got out of the wheelbarrow, they both thanked Fudge for the ride around the garden. 'But now we have to go back indoors, and you should go back into your enclosure, too, Fudge,' said Andrew.

The kids lead the gorilla back to the entrance of his enclosure, and big old Fudge went back inside, making deep sounds as he moved. Andrew closed the door and locked it, then said to Fudge, 'hey, Fudge, we'll be back to see you tomorrow night, okay?'

The big ape seemed to understand Andrew, he made a few more huffing sounds, then disappeared back inside his enclosure.

'Come on, Gem, we don't want to get caught,' said Andrew, and the kids went back inside their house, so happy that they had had an amazing night.

Chapter Seven

It was now Monday morning, but as it was the summer holiday, Andrew and Gemma had no school to rush off to. In fact, it was about eight-thirty when Andrew and Gemma stumbled into the dining room for breakfast.

'Oh, there you two are,' said their nan, 'you two sleepy heads are up, then, are you?'

'Yes, Grandma,' mumbled Andrew, still half asleep.

'And what would you two little lambs like for breakfast, eh?'

Gemma thought about it for a few seconds, then said, 'can I have some strawberry jam on toast, please, Grandma?'

'Yes, of course, you can, sweetheart,' said their nan.

'I'll have marmalade on toast, please, nan,' said Andrew.

'Right, you are then, young man, and I'll make a fresh pot of tea for us all,' replied their grandma.

The children's grandad was reading his newspaper, at one end of the table, 'you whippersnappers don't know you're born, I bet you're up half the night?' For a second Andrew and Gemma glanced at each other, Andrew was worried that their grandad had found out.

'What do you mean, Grandad?' said Andrew, tentatively.

'I know what you young 'uns get up to, at night.'

Andrew gulped, and said, 'you do?'

'Yes, you little tykes are probably up half the night, playing your Gameboy's and Nintendo's, or whatever you call 'um, these days, aren't you?' said their grandad.

'Oh, yeah, that's right, Grandad,' said Andrew, relieved.

Just then, Grandad's mobile rang, Grandad heard it and tried to locate where he had left it. 'Now, where did I leave that damn thing?' murmured Grandad to himself.

'It's on the mantelpiece, Grandad,' said Gemma.

'On, yes, so it is, thanks, pet,' said Grandad. He picked it up and answered it, 'hello.' It was Andrew's mum, she was calling to see how the kids were, and what time she should come round and collect them?

'Oh, I don't know, really,' said Grandad to Andrew's mum, 'I'll ask them, 'cause they are here with me, having breakfast.' Andrew's grandad turned to face the children, and said, 'hey, you two, it's your mum on the phone, she wants to know what time to come round and pick you up?'

Gemma looked at Andrew, and Andrew looked at his sister, they both looked a bit worried; they had forgotten that they were only scheduled to stay for the weekend.

'But we don't want to go back, yet, Grandad,' said Andrew.

'Can we stay a few more days, please, Grandad?' said young Gemma.

Their grandad smiled at them, and said, 'well, it's alright with me, but let me check with your mum.'

Grandad asked the children's mother if it was okay if they stayed a few more days. The kid's mum said that they could, as long as it was okay with Grandad and Nan.

'Yeah, it's fine with me, love, it really is; the children have been good as gold,' said Grandad to Gemma's mother. 'Yes, of course, I will,' continued Grandad, 'a few more nights then, right you are, look forward to it, see you then, bye, love,' and then he ended the call.

'Right then,' said Grandad to Andrew and Gemma, 'we've got a few more days together.'

The kids both raised their arms in the air together, and shouted, 'YEAH!'

Just then, Andrew's nan walked back into the dining room, with a fresh pot of tea, and said, 'what's the cheering about?'

'Well, that was their mum on the phone,' said Grandad, 'she said the kids can stay a few more days with us, if that's alright with us. I told her it's okay.'

'Yes, of course, it's alright,' replied Grandma. 'Now I've got a busy day today because I'm heading round to Cynthia's, remember I told you yesterday?' said, Grandma.

'Oh, yeah, I forgot, something about a film, isn't it?'

'Yes love,' said Grandma, 'I'm going over to Cynthia's to watch a couple of films; musical films today, the wizard of Oz, and the sound of music. Now, remember, I also told you that Rosemary is going over there too, and we're both staying the night.'

'Yes, yes, I've got it now,' answered Grandad.

'So, you'll be on your own with the Grandkids most of the day, and this evening,' said Nan. She looked at her grandkids, and said, 'you two make sure you behave well for your grandad, won't you?'

'Yes, we will, Grandma,' replied Andrew, he then glanced at Gemma and smirked, after all, they did have a pretty good secret between them.

'Can we watch cartoons on the cartoon channel after breakfast, Grandad?' asked Gemma.

'Yes, you can, pet, but make sure you both eat your breakfast first, and don't have the volume up too loud 'cause that's annoying,'

'Okay, Grandad,' said Andrew.

After the children had watched cartoons for an hour, they got into their grandad's car, with their nan too. Grandad was taking Grandma over to Cynthia's house to watch movies; but first, they headed to the supermarket, so Andrew's nan could buy a big box of chocolates, for her friend to eat whilst watching the movies.

In the supermarket, Andrew whispered to Gemma, 'hey, Gem, why don't you ask Grandma if she'll let us have some Pick N Mix?'

'That's a good idea, Andrew,' said Gemma. Gemma's grandma was in a good mood, so she let the children get a cup of Pick N Mix each. Gemma walked up to Andrew and whispered, 'we have to save some sweets for big Fudge.'

'Yes, you're right, Gem, we do,' replied Andrew, excitedly.

After a short while, the family had left the supermarket, and were on their way to Cynthia's house. Before long, they had arrived there and said goodbye to their lovely grandmother.

On the way back, Grandad suddenly remembered a horse race that he wanted to place a bet on. They drove to the high street, parked-up, then Grandad said to the kids, 'now you two wait in the car; I'll only be five minutes, don't go anywhere, understand?'

'Yes, Grandad, we'll stay right here,' mumbled Andrew, eating a mouthful of sweets. While their grandad was in the betting shop, Andrew and Gemma talked about what they wanted to do during the night, with big Fudge,

'We could try to teach the gorilla how to cartwheel?' said young Gemma.

Andrew thought about that, for a few seconds, then said, 'yeah, maybe, but that would probably be too difficult.'

Andrew thought about what they could do, then said, 'I want to see big Fudge climb a tree, yeah that would be great to see.'

'Yes, that would be fun to see,' replied his sister. 'Or we could put Fudge in goal, and take shots at him, he'd probably be really good as a goalie.'

'Yes, yes, maybe we could do that, too,' said Andrew.

Just then, their grandad came back to the car, so the kids had to end their conversation. Grandad got back in the driver's seat, and said, 'that's that little job done.' He started up the car and drove away, then he said, 'you know there's cricket on the TV this afternoon, that I want to watch, test cricket at that, England versus Bangladesh.'

'We don't have to watch it, do we, Grandad?' said Andrew. 'It's just that it's a bit boring.'

'Well, if it's not your cup of tea, you can do something else to entertain yourself; as long as you two behave yourself,' said Grandad. 'Read your books,' their grandad said, 'books are good for you; reading broadens the mind.'

'So, why don't you read one of your books, then, Grandad?' enquired little Gemma.

'Because I'll be watching the cricket, you see, love, and cricket is also good for you,' and with that, Grandad chuckled to himself.

The afternoon passed by with Grandad drinking tea, and watching his beloved cricket; England had batted well, they were all out for 569 runs. Grandad was very pleased with this, 'this should be a winning score,' he said to himself.

Gemma spent most of the afternoon playing with her doll and reading books on fairy-tales; Andrew played his gaming console and did some reading.

When dinner time arrived, Grandad surprised his grandkids, by saying, 'Hey you two little pups, I don't fancy cooking tonight, and seeing how your Nan is away, why don't I order us a pizza?'

'YEAH!' shouted Gemma. 'I love pizza.'

'Me too!' shouted Andrew. 'I want Pepperoni.'

Their grandad laughed, 'Okay, I'll get you a large Pepperoni one, and how about you?' said grandad, looking at young Gemma.

'Can I have the one with a pineapple on it?' answered Gemma.

'Hawaiian, that one's called Hawaiian,' said Andrew.

'Right you are, then,' said Grandad, 'I'll order two large pizzas, and I'll have a slice or two of both of you.'

Chapter Eight

The clock in Andrew's bedroom said ten minutes to midnight, and young Andrew Tyler was ready once again; ready for fun and adventure. Andrew could actually feel his body tingle with nervous energy, it was excitement, the prospect of pure fun and thrills that lay ahead.

Once again, Andrew opened his bedroom door, quietly, once again, he listened for any sounds in the house. Andrew was getting used to this routine, he imagined he was a secret agent, on another night-time mission.

Gemma opened her bedroom door, before Andrew had time to reach it; she was getting good at this prowling around the house, lark, too.

Downstairs in the kitchen, Andrew said to Gemma, 'I want to feed Fudge, honey.'

'Don't forget, we have Pick N Mix,' said Gemma.

'I know we have, but the gorilla will love honey too, I'm sure of it,' replied Andrew.

Andrew went to one of the cupboards in the kitchen and took out a jar of Sainsbury's Honey. The kids grabbed the keys that they needed, and a couple of minutes later, were outside Fudge's enclosure.

'Gem, you take the lid of the jar of honey, and leave it on the ground, with the bag of Pick N Mix,' said Andrew. 'I'll open the door, while you're doing that.'

Gemma tried to take the lid of the honey jar, but couldn't get it off. 'I can't get the lid off, Andrew,' she said.

'Okay, let me try, then,' whispered Andrew, the boy took hold of the honey jar, and with some considerable effort, opened the jar. 'There, I've done it, Gem, I just hope he likes it now,' said Andrew.

With the sweets and honey in the right place, the enclosure door was opened, and out walked the giant ape, the gorilla huffed and sniffed the air, big Fudge looked at Andrew and Gemma and huffed deep sounds, the gorilla's way of saying hello.

'Hi, Fudge, how are you?' said Andrew.

'We've brought you more goodies,' said Gemma. The ape knuckled-walked over to the honey jar, he sniffed the jar with his broad, flat nose. Then he dipped a finger into the honey, sniffed it again, and then ate the honey.

Big Fudge seemed to really like the honey, he started to get excited, his large body started to move up and down, whilst standing on all fours. The gorilla then placed two fingers in the honey jar and scooped up a large dollop of golden honey; then he stuck his fingers in his mouth and sucked the honey from his fingers.

Huffing deep sounds, the gorilla was clearly getting more excited. 'He loves the honey, Gemma, look at him,' said Andrew. Then Fudge noticed the Pick N Mix sweets, he sniffed the sweets, then picked up one of the sweets, and ate it.

Clearly, the gorilla loved it, he then took a large handful of sweets and shovelled them into his mouth. Gemma and Andrew laughed out loud when they saw this, 'he loves the sweets too, Andrew,' said Gemma.

Big Fudge sat there for a minute chewing the sweets, and making eating noises with his mouth. Then the big ape decided it was time to move around the garden, like before; it was time to stretch his legs.

As the gorilla moved quicker around the lawn, he started to beat his chest, this he did in short percussive bursts, with his hands. Andrew and his sister laughed again, 'hey, Gem, that is the sound I heard that day in the garden, remember?'

'Yes, I remember,' replied Gemma, Fudge loved being free, he ran up to the garden fence and peered over. Suddenly, Fudge started to climb the fence post, it was a concrete post, so it could take his weight.

Next thing, he was over the fence, and running around the neighbour's garden. The children looked over the fence and laughed, Andrew had to lift young Gemma up, as she was only six.

Fudge made deep hooting and huffing sounds as he moved, then he headed for the clothesline, he ran straight into a big, white, bed sheet.

The white sheet covered the ape, so now, he looked like a ghost, flying around the lawn; this made Gemma and her brother crack up. Then the gorilla got the sheet off, and ran back towards the washing line, he knocked off a pair of jeans, which for a few seconds, wrapped around his neck.

Then the big gorilla ran round in a big circle again, and back towards the washing line. Suddenly, Fudge got a pair of old lady bloomers stuck on his head; he ran towards a shed that was next to the back of their neighbour's house.

The ape jumped up onto the roof of the shed, then he jumped up onto the windowsill of the upstairs bedroom. The gorilla huffed and puffed at the window, then the curtains were drawn back, and an old lady looked out the window.

The elderly lady got frightened when she saw a gorilla, looking through her window, with a pair of bloomers on his head. 'Ahh!' The old lady screamed, the elderly lady in question was Mrs Davis, a neighbour and friend of Andrew's grandparents.

Big Fudge jumped down onto the roof of the garden shed, nearly breaking it with his weight. He then ran back to the fence that divided the two gardens, and climbed back up the fence post, and hurried over to the kids.

The children were still laughing, Andrew approached the gorilla and pulled the pair of bloomers off his big head, Fudge looked confused. 'We better get Fudge back into his enclosure,' said Andrew to Gemma.

'Yes, quickly,' replied Gemma, Andrew opened the door to the enclosure, and big Fudge went back inside. Andrew locked the enclosure door, then looked up at the neighbour's window, the light was on. 'Come on, Gem, we better get back inside.'

Chapter Nine

News and gossip spread fast around neighbourhoods. This was the next morning, the morning after the night of antics and mayhem; at least that's how poor Mrs Davis saw things. She had already told the neighbour who lived on the other side of her, Mrs Lawrence.

Mrs Davis had told Mrs Lawrence how she had been asleep, when she heard noises outside, in the back garden, 'strange goings-on,' was how she put it. Mrs Davis continued with her account, she said that after hearing sounds in the garden, she got up to take a look.

She pulled back her bedroom curtains, and was confronted with, 'the strangest thing I ever saw.'

Mrs Davis said that she was sure that she saw a big gorilla outside her bedroom window. '—not only a big gorilla, but the thing was wearing a pair of bloomers on his head.'

'And you hadn't been drinking, June?' enquired Mrs Lawrence.

'Not a drop, love, I was as sober as a judge when I went to bed, let me tell you. In fact, I haven't had a drop since my birthday, and that was two months ago.'

Mrs Davis continued, 'just tea, love, PG Tips, that was all, and you can't get drunk on PG Tips.'

'But where did it come from? How did it get here?' asked Mrs Lawrence.

'Well, old Alex Tyler keeps animals, doesn't he,' continued Mrs Davis, 'I know he's got some exotic animals in his menagerie, but he hasn't got a gorilla. I know he's got one of those Reddy, pig things, what do you call 'um?'

'And he's got those funny looking monkeys from South America, Marmite monkeys, something like that,' added Mrs Lawrence.

'Yes, but nothing like a gorilla, surely?' said Mrs Davis. 'But this morning I went outside to have a look, and low and behold, what I saw in the back garden?'

'Don't tell me you saw the gorilla?' said Mrs Lawrence.

'No, but all my washing from my washing line was scattered all over the garden.'

'Really? I don't believe it,' said Mrs Lawrence.

'And not only that,' continued Mrs Davis, 'but a pair of my bloomers were missing. I'd only bought them a month before, at Marks and Spencers, as well.'

'So, you didn't dream it, after all,' added Mrs Lawrence.

'No. Not with that sort of mess in my back garden, I never left it like that, did I?' replied Mrs Davis, exasperated.

'Well, there's only one thing for it,' said Mrs Lawrence, 'you're gonna have to call the police, aren't you?'

'You know what, Betty, I think you're right, I'm going to report this.'

Andrew was looking out of his bedroom window, he could see clothes and a big white sheet strewn across the lawn. Big Fudge did make a right mess in that garden, thought Andrew. 'Still, it was funny, especially when Fudge climbed up to that window,' Andrew murmured to himself.

Andrew left his bedroom to go and find his sister, she was downstairs eating her breakfast of Crunchy Nut Cornflakes.

Andrew walked into the dining room and said, 'morning, Gem, where's Grandad?'

'He's outside feeding his animals,' replied Gemma.

'Have you seen next door's garden? It's a right mess from Fudge.'

'It is?' replied Gemma.

'Yeah, it is, but it was well funny, though, wasn't it?' said Andrew.

'Yes, it was very funny,' said his sister. Gemma suddenly looked very serious, 'but do you think we'll get into trouble?'

'Get into trouble? It wasn't our fault; it was the gorilla.'

'But we let him out,' said Gemma, sounding worried.

'Yeah, we let him out of his cage, but what he does after that, is up to him,' said Andrew, somewhat defiantly. 'Look, we're only having fun, we're not hurting anyone, are we?'

'But what if the woman next door complains?' said Gemma.

'Well, we don't want to get into trouble, do we? So we'll just pretend to know nothing about it,' said Andrew, confidently.

'Are we going to go out in the back garden again, tonight? Enquired Gemma.

'You bet we are, playing with a big gorilla in the garden at night is great fun, isn't it? I've never had so much fun,' added Andrew; 'and it's secret fun and adventure because we're the only ones who know about it.'

'But what if we get caught, we'll be in so much trouble with Grandad?' asked Gemma, worried once again.

'You know what, Gem, you worry too much, 'cause we're not gonna get caught,' answered Andrew, trying hard to reassure his sister.

Just then the children heard the back door to the kitchen open, it was Grandad coming back inside, after feeding his animals. Andrew looked at Gemma, and said, 'Now remember, Gem, not a word, no matter what; it's our amazing secret, okay?'

Gemma nodded, and then their grandad walked into the dining room, 'Morning kids, how are you two little munchkins today?'

'Morning Grandad,' replied Andrew, 'we're fine, thanks.'

'That's good to hear, you can tell Grandma that I'm not entirely useless, when I bring her back soon,' said their grandad.

'Are we going with you to pick her up?' asked Gemma.

'Well, I was going to take you both, but your Nan rang me earlier, and told me she was bringing Cynthia back with her. Cynthia and your Nan are gonna do some more baking this afternoon, and Cynthia will also be staying the night,' said Grandad.

'So Andrew, young man, I need you to look after your sister, for an hour or so, while I go and pick the ladies up, okay?' asked Grandad.

'Yes, Grandad, we can watch TV together,' answered Andrew.

'Good lad, you know you two are great kids, you're no trouble at all, I'll tell your mum and dad about how well you've behaved,' said Grandad.

'Thank you, Grandad,' said Gemma.

'Right O, I'm heading off, now, okay? I won't be long,' and with that, Grandad left the house.

Chapter Ten

Andrew and his sister were enjoying watching cartoons when there was a ring of the doorbell. Andrew looked at Gemma and said, 'I wonder who that is?' Andrew got off the sofa and went to open the front door, he opened it, and saw a stern-faced, elderly lady, Mrs Davis; the next-door neighbour.

'Hello,' said Andrew, Mrs Davis looked at him and said, 'I'm June from next door, is Alex or Joyce in?'

'No, they're both out at the moment, but will be back later,' replied Andrew.

'Are they? Well, maybe you heard something? It's about last night; something very strange was going on in my back garden,' said Mrs Davis.

'Your back garden?' said Andrew, a bit nervously.

'Yes, my back garden,' continued Mrs Davis, 'a right carry on, let me tell you.'

'What?' enquired Andrew.

'Yes, last night, monkey business going on, scared me to death, in the middle of the night. Did you hear anything?' asked Mrs Davis.

'No, er, I, no I didn't hear anything unusual,' mumbled Andrew, nervously, 'why, what happened?'

'A GORILLA! That's what happened,' said Mrs Davis, loudly.

'A gorilla? Where?' asked Andrew.

'That's what I'm trying to tell you, in my back garden, there was a gorilla in my garden.'

'Wow, there was?' said Andrew, pretending to be surprised.

'Yes, there was, I saw the great big, hairy thing, he was looking through my bedroom window,' stated Mrs Davis. 'And the police won't believe me.'

'They won't?' asked Andrew.

'No I've just been on the phone to them, they told me it couldn't have been a gorilla; because gorilla's don't live in suburbia. The police told me to stop wasting their time.'

'They did?' said Andrew.

'Yes, the cheek of it, I told him, I did, I told that officer I spoke to, that I don't ever waste the police's time. That I wasn't dreaming or drunk, that I've been outside in the back garden, and my washing line is all over the place.'

'But the police said it's probably teenagers in a fancy dress costume, mucking about at night,' continued Mrs Davis. 'They told me they haven't got time to look into wild goose chases, I told them I am not talking about a wild goose chase, I'm talking about a wild gorilla on the loose.'

'So what are you going to do now?' asked Andrew.

'I really don't know,' answered Mrs Davis, 'I'm going to go and talk to your neighbour next door, Ted Reynolds, to see if he heard or saw anything. And then I think I'll call the council, they should be able to do something for me, at least.'

Then Mrs Davis started to walk away, 'you tell your grandparents that I'll be back round to see them, at some point,' said Mrs Davis, as she walked up the garden path.

'Okay I will,' said Andrew, then he closed the front door. Gemma was standing by Andrew when he turned around, 'did you hear that, Gem?'

'Yes, I did, what are we gonna do?'

'Well, I'll tell our grandparents that Mrs Davis called round, but I won't mention anything about a gorilla,' said Andrew.

'But the neighbour said she saw a gorilla, Andrew,' said Gemma, rather worried.

'She also said that the police didn't believe her and that they thought it was teenagers, mucking about at night. We can say the same thing to Grandad, when he gets back,' said Andrew.

About forty minutes later, Andrew and Gemma were still watching cartoons on TV, and eating crisps and drinking Cola, when they heard their grandparents arrive outside.

A minute later their grandmother let herself in, with her key, followed by her friend, Cynthia, and then their grandad. 'Hello kids,' said Nan, 'everything okay?'

'Yes, thanks, Nan,' said Gemma.

'Cynthia is here to do some baking with me today,' said Andrew's Nan.

'Hello there, kids, how are you two?' asked Cynthia.

'Hi, Cynthia,' said Andrew.

'Hello, Cynthia,' said young Gemma. The children's Nan had a bag of shopping with her, ingredients mostly, for the cakes that they were going to bake, that afternoon. 'Let me put this little lot away, then make us a nice cup of tea; you make yourself at home, Cynthia,' said Joyce.

'Thank you, Joyce,' replied Cynthia. Gemma's grandma busied herself in the kitchen, getting cups and saucers ready, and placing tea bags in the teapot. She also started putting shopping away, as she did so, Gemma came into the kitchen and started helping her Nan.

'You are a right little angel, Gemma, aren't you?' said, Grandma.

'Grandma,' said Gemma, 'your neighbour just called round to see you, a little while ago.'

'My neighbour? Who do you mean, Ted or June?'

'Mrs Davis,' said Gemma.

'Oh, June, what did she want?' asked Grandma.

'She wanted to tell you that there was a bit of a disturbance in her back garden last night,' said Gemma.

'A bit of a disturbance? From what?' enquired their Nan.

'Well, I think she said—'

'She said teenagers got into her back garden last night, and were running around,' interrupted Andrew.

'Teenagers?' said Grandma. 'Last night? Well, did you hear anything? Still, it doesn't surprise me, this neighbourhood is usually quite quiet, but when you read about what goes on, you just never know these days, do you?' continued Grandma.

'What's this about teenagers?' said Grandad, walking into the kitchen.

'The kids said June from next door, had teenagers running around her back garden last night, did you hear anything, love?' said Grandma.

'No, but we're both heavy sleepers, I didn't hear anything out of the ordinary,' said Grandad.

'I hope she wasn't too scared by them,' said Grandma Joyce, reflectively, 'well, anyway, let's go into the living room and have some tea and cakes. And afterwards, Cynthia and I want the kitchen to ourselves, so we can bake, okay?'

Chapter Eleven

'Come to think of it, June, I did hear something weird, outside last night; noises coming from the back gardens,' said Ted Reynolds, the neighbour who lived on the other side of Grandad Tyler.

'I'm telling ya, Ted, I've never seen the likes of it in my life,' said June Davis. 'I don't care if the police won't believe me, I'm telling you, it WAS a gorilla,' said Mrs Davis. 'It means I'm not stupid or senile, it looked too real, too life-like, to be a costume, surely,' continued Mrs Davis.

'But these days, June, the costumes that are out there are quite realistic, I've seen them on TV,' said Ted.

'Yes, but I saw movement in his face, in his eyes, I'm sure it really was a gorilla, looking in on me,' said Mrs Davis.

'If the Old Bill won't believe you,' said Ted, 'then get on to the council; they can send an environmental health officer, or someone like that, to look into it, for you.'

'I mean, what if the great, big thing comes back? I'm on my own, after all, I don't have Henry anymore to protect me, do I? Not after he passed away,' said Mrs Davis.

Ted thought of something to say to try to console Mrs Davis, 'I'm sure you won't ever see that thing again, June, no he's long gone; I mean, he's not gonna stick around, is he? No, you'll never see his big hairy, body again, so you don't have to worry yourself.'

While Mrs Davis was talking to Ted Reynolds, back in the Tyler household, Grandma Joyce and her friend Cynthia, were baking cakes.

Today they were baking three cakes: Blueberry, fruit and strawberry. Two were for their local church for afternoon tea and cakes for everyone there, and one was for the Tyler family.

The three cake-mixes had all been mixed and poured into the baking tins, and now Grandma Joyce was loading them into the oven. 'You know, Cynthia, I love this part about baking,' said Grandma Joyce.

'I know what you're going to say,' said Cynthia, then both women said together, 'the best thing about baking is licking the leftover cake mix from the baking bowls.' Then both women laughed.

'And I've got lovely, thick, cream to put on top of the cakes, lovely, delicious, Vanilla cream,' added Grandma Joyce.

'You're just too kind, Joyce,' said Cynthia.

'That's another six!' shouted Andrew's grandad, 'I've still got the touch.' Andrew, Gemma and their grandad were at their local park, having fun together playing cricket.

'But can't I stand behind you, Grandad, and catch the balls you miss?' said Gemma.

You mean play Wicket Keeper,' replied Grandad, 'no I want you out there, way over there to my right, fielding.'

'But I can't catch the balls you hit at me!' shouted Gemma to her grandad.

'You'll get better at catching the tennis ball, the more you practice,' shouted back Grandad.

'Come on Grandad,' shouted Andrew, 'get ready; I'm ready to bowl again.'

'Okay, young man,' said Grandad,' try to bowl me out, if you can,' Grandad chuckled to himself. Andrew took a big run-up, and bowled the tennis ball as best he could, trying to bowl like the cricketers on TV do.

The ball came hurtling towards Grandad, he allowed for the ball to bounce twice, instead of once, as Andrew was only a little boy. Then Grandad was able to get a decent contact on the ball once again, with good swinging action, and follow-through.

The ball rose high into the sky, Gemma ran to try and catch it, but she couldn't get there in time; then the tennis ball bounced over Gemma, and kept ongoing.

'That's a boundary, any day,' shouted Grandad, the ball ended up coming to a stop next to a park bench. The park bench was under an old Oak tree, and sitting on the bench was the same, elderly, lady that Andrew and Gemma had met the last time they were at the park.

'Hello, my dear,' said the elderly lady to Gemma, 'fancy meeting you again.'

'Hello,' said Gemma, 'how are you?'

'I'm just fine, thank you, my lovely,' answered the elderly lady. 'I see you're playing cricket with your brother and Grandad, are you enjoying it?'

Gemma thought about the question for a few seconds, then she scrunched up her nose, and said, 'I am enjoying it, but I can't catch the ball very often; Grandad keeps hitting the ball too high and too far.'

'Do you want to have a little fun with your grandad?' asked the elderly lady.

'What kind of fun?' enquired young Gemma.

'Shall we attach some colourful balloons to your grandad's cricket bat, while he's playing cricket?'

Gemma laughed and threw her arms up in the air, and shouted 'yeah!'

Let's do that, but how can you do that?'

'It's magic, my dear, simply magic,' replied the nice, elderly lady.

The elderly lady smiled at Gemma, and said, 'Now you run along and throw the ball back to your brother, then we can watch him bowl to your grandad. But this time, I think his cricket bat will look a little different,' then the elderly lady laughed.

Gemma picked up the tennis ball, turned around and ran toward Andrew, after running a few yards, Gemma threw the ball to her brother; the ball didn't quite reach him, but it went close enough.

Andrew picked up the ball, then he began his run-up to bowl, he was determined to bowl his grandad out this time. Andrew bowled, but just as his grandad was about to hit the ball, he stopped, as he realised his cricket bat was full of multi-coloured balloons.

Gemma started to laugh, and Andrew began to laugh too, then even Grandad started laughing. 'How bizarre?' said Grandad. 'What in the name of God?'

'Grandad, Grandad!' shouted Gemma, 'your cricket bat is covered in balloons.'

'I can see that, but how?' asked Grandad, confused. Young Gemma turned around, and looked at the elderly lady, the lady smiled at Gemma, and Gemma smiled back.

Grandad was still scratching his head, wondering how those balloons had got attached to his cricket bat, as he and the children enjoyed delicious ice-creams, once again.

'Maybe it's magic,' said Gemma to her grandad, her grandad looked down at her, and smiled and said, 'well, maybe it is, young Gemma, maybe it is.'

Chapter Twelve

'The midnight hour had rolled around, once again, and we know what that means don't we?' Andrew was talking quietly to Gemma in her bedroom. 'Yes, I've just heard Cynthia snoring in her bedroom, as I left my bedroom, to come and get you,' said Andrew.

'But we still have to be as quiet as mice, Gem,' whispered Andrew to his sister.

'I know,' whispered back Gemma. The kids left Gemma's bedroom as quietly as they could, crept along the landing, paused at the top of the stairs to listen for any sounds; the coast was clear.

As the children crept into the kitchen, they both noticed, straight away, three very nice looking cakes, covered in cream. 'Wow,' whispered Andrew, 'it's like a cake shop in here.'

A few seconds later, Andrew was locking the back door behind him, 'Now let's go and see Fudge,' said Andrew to his sister, whose smile was big and bright.

'Fudge, Fudge,' said Andrew, through the opening of the Gorilla's enclosure, then a few seconds later, big Fudge appeared at the opening. The big gorilla started to get excited when he heard and saw the children, Fudge began to huff deeply, and started swaying his large body about. He also lifted his huge arms up in the air, almost like a football supporter, when his team scores a goal.

Andrew unlocked the enclosure, and the big ape came out, 'hi, Fudge,' said Gemma. The gorilla scooped-up Andrew and Gemma and hugged them. Andrew laughed out loud, and so did his sister, big Fudge huffed and grunted, doing his best to communicate with the children.

Andrew wondered if the ape was ticklish, so he started to tickle Fudge, the gorilla reacted to the tickles, huffing repeatedly, like gorilla laughter. Big Fudge seemed to like being tickled by Andrew, he rolled over on the grass, lying on his back with his legs up in the air.

Gemma and Andrew laughed at Fudge's reaction, 'hey look, Gemma, he likes it,' said Andrew. Then Fudge sat up and motioned with his hand that he wanted some sweets.

'I don't have any sweets for you, tonight, Fudge,' said Andrew; 'we can't get sweets every night, because we're not allowed them every night, you see.' Andrew hoped that the big ape understood.

But then Fudge sniffed the air, he had caught the scent or smell of something, he sniffed some more; then he started to follow his nose. 'He can smell something, Gemma,' said Andrew, as the kids followed the gorilla down the garden.

'He's heading towards the house,' said Gemma.

'I wonder what he can smell?' replied Andrew. Onwards went big Fudge, knuckle-walking down the lawn, then the ape reached the back door of Andrew's grandparent's house.

The gorilla sniffed at the door, then he started huffing, once again, the gorilla's hand brushed against the door, indicating to the kids that he wanted to go inside the house.

'It must be the cakes he can smell,' said Andrew, 'I'm going to open the door, and get Fudge a big slice of cake.' Young Gemma didn't say anything, just nodded her head in agreement.

Andrew took the key out of his pocket, placed it in the lock, turned the key, and unlocked the back door; he then turned the handle, quietly and slowly, and opened the back door.

Suddenly, the large ape pushed his way inside, he pushed Andrew out of the way and picked up one of the cakes. Then Fudge took a big bite out of the cake and got a face full of thick cream.

'No Fudge, wait!' said Andrew. 'You can't eat it all,' but it was too late, the gorilla took a huge handful of cake and shovelled it into his mouth. Then Fudge buried his face into the cake, to scoff as much as he could.

The ape looked at Andrew and Gemma, his face was white with cream all over it, then the gorilla huffed a few times, and then went back outside, into the garden.

Big Fudge was getting more excited by the minute, he beat his chest and huffed some more. Then the big gorilla started running around the garden, still with his face covered in white cream.

'He must be experiencing a sugar rush,' said Andrew to his sister, 'the type mum goes on about when she doesn't want us to have too much sugar.'

By now the ape was full of energy, he raced around the garden in big circles, whilst the children looked on. Fudge started to climb a tree that was next to the fence of his neighbour's garden, Ted Reynolds.

Up and up went the great ape, higher and higher into the tree; then the gorilla started to swing, by hanging on to a large branch, that grew near Ted's house.

Fudge moved along the branch, left hand then right hand, then left again, until he was close to Ted's bedroom window. Fudge swung and grabbed the brick recess just below Ted Reynold's window, now he was holding on to the brickwork, with both hands.

The gorilla still had cream all over his face, Andrew and Gemma looked on, open-mouthed, big Fudge made more huffing and grunting noises, then suddenly the bedroom light came on.

Next thing the curtains flew open, and a man looked out the window, it was their neighbour Ted. 'Ahhh!' said Ted. 'What in god's name is that?' The gorilla was looking through Ted's window, ghostly white-faced and frightening.

Big Fudge made more animalistic sounds and stared through the window at Ted, poor Ted couldn't believe his eyes, he looked like he had seen a ghost; 'oh my—' but Ted couldn't finish what he was trying to say, because he fainted instead.

Chapter Thirteen

Big Fudge the gorilla was climbing back down the tree next to Ted Reynold's garden, the ape was still excited, and hyperactive. 'Fudge, Fudge, come back over here,' said Andrew, hoping the great ape would, somehow, understand him.

Fudge looked over at the children, huffed at them, and then went over to them. Andrew looked up at Ted's window, he could see the light was on, and the curtains were open; but he didn't know that their neighbour had just fainted with fright.

'We have to get out of here,' said Andrew. The gorilla looked at Andrew, then Gemma said, 'but where can we go?' Just as Gemma asked that question, a light came on in the house next door to Ted's house.

'If we stay in the back garden, someone could see us,' said Andrew, then Andrew had the answer, 'I know, we can go up onto the roofs, that way no one will be able to see us.'

Andrew and young Gemma climbed onto the back of Fudge, and held on to his long hair. 'Up, up you go Fudge, climb on to the roofs,' said Andrew, the gorilla understood what Andrew wanted, he made some deep, animalistic sounds, once again; then started to climb back up the same tree as before.

From an out-lying branch, it was easy for the great ape to climb onto the roof of Ted Reynold's house. Andrew and Gemma held on to Fudge, tightly, as the gorilla knuckle-walked along the roof of houses.

It was a nice, warm night, and the children were tingling with excitement – they were having the adventure of a lifetime. There was a full moon and thousands of stars were out, a galaxy of wonder and awe.

Fudge continued knuckle-walking along the rooftops that made up the neighbourhood. Soon the gorilla and the children reached the end of the street, but that was no problem to a big, strong gorilla; Fudge simply jumped across onto a nearby tree branch, then jumped onto another roof, and continued on his way.

From a back bedroom window, a certain elderly lady saw the gorilla and Andrew and Gemma, riding on his back. It was the magical lady from the park, she smiled when she saw them, then waved her hand like a wand, in their direction.

Suddenly the big ape, Andrew and Gemma too, had a balloon tied to them; one balloon each. 'Andrew, look,' said Gemma, 'we each have a balloon,' Andrew looked and noticed the balloons.

'Where did these balloons come from?' he asked.

'That nice old lady must have noticed us, and given us a balloon each,' replied young Gemma. As they all got closer to the local park, the big gorilla and the children were silhouetted against the full disk of the yellow moon, with the balloons clearly visible too; as they moved across the rooftops.

After a short while they reached the park, 'I know what we should do,' said Gemma.

'What?' enquired Andrew.

'We should make a wish,' said his sister.

Andrew looked a little bemused for a second, then asked, 'What kind of wish?'

'We should wish to always stay together,' said Gemma.

'Let's release our balloons to make the wish official,' said Andrew, little Gemma untied her balloon, and held on to it, Andrew untied his balloon, 'Gem, hold on to my balloon for a second, while I untie Fudge's balloon.'

Gemma held her brother's balloon while Andrew untied the balloon that was around the gorilla. 'Okay ready, but let Fudge hold his balloon too,' said Andrew.

Gemma handed the balloon to big Fudge, the ape took the balloon in his large hand, held it by the string, and he then sniffed the balloon. 'Right,' said Andrew, 'let's release our balloons on the count of three.'

'Okay, then,' said Gemma.

'I'll count the numbers, one, two...three!' shouted out Andrew, and with that, all three balloons lifted up into the night sky, as the children made their special wish.

Up sailed the three balloons, higher and higher, silently floating away, like dreams from one's imagination. Even the big gorilla watched the balloons climbing higher into the night sky, then he huffed two short huffs; which meant he was getting excited again.

Then, Andrew suddenly realised something: 'you know what?'

'What?' said his sister.

'We've got the whole park to ourselves,' said Andrew, excitedly. 'I know what we should do, let's run around, let's race each other through the park.'

'Okay,' said Gemma, 'go!' And then the kids started to run as fast as they could, heading deeper into the dark, empty park. The children were shouting out, 'YEAH!' As they ran through the empty park, they were zigzagging between each other, and even the gorilla joined in.

Then Andrew started doing cartwheels, and so his sister started to copy him too, 'look at me, Andrew,' trying to out-do her brother. Then big Fudge started doing cartwheels as well, and it turned out, that the ape was better at doing cartwheels than the kids were.

Gemma started laughing at the gorilla doing cartwheels, and then Andrew started laughing, he laughed so much that he crashed to the ground.

'I want to sit down and rest,' said Gemma. Andrew looked around, then noticed a park bench under a park lamp; not far from where they had stopped.

'Let's go and sit on that bench, over there,' said Andrew.

All that running around had left the kids out of breath, and even Fudge seemed to be breathing heavily. 'It's so quiet here, isn't it?' said Andrew.

'Yes, it's so different compared to the daytime,' replied Gemma. After the gorilla had rested for a few minutes, he found a few sticks to play with. The gorilla held a stick in his hand and tapped it on the ground, by the park bench.

Fudge tapped the stick several times, producing a simple rhythm. The big ape tapped the stick to his left side, then to his right side. Then Andrew picked up a stick and started tapping in time with the gorilla's beat. Gemma laughed at what she saw and heard but didn't want to be left out, so she picked-up another stick, and joined in with the other two.

Now, Andrew, Gemma and Fudge were all tapping their sticks in unison, tap-tap-tap-tap, then tap-tap-tap-tap. Then the gorilla stood up on his legs and continued drumming the same beat; Andrew and Gemma joined him, one on each side of the gorilla.

Tap-tap-tap-tap and tap-tap-tap-tap, all three of them were directly under the full beam of the park lamp. Next, they all started swaying left and right as they continued playing their rhythm; they looked like performers on a West-End stage.

Then Andrew pointed his stick on the ground and started to dance in a big circle; Gemma and Fudge followed his lead. Then Andrew tapped his stick on the park lamp post, one, two, three, four, tap-tap-tap-tap, then the gorilla drummed out the same beat; then Gemma played out exactly the same rhythm.

'This is good fun,' said Andrew, 'this is like a music lesson at school, only much more enjoyable.'

'Oi! You lot! What do you think you're playing at?' the voice rang out of the darkness, the children and the ape, all suddenly, stopped what they were doing.

'The park is closed, get out of it!' said the voice; it was the Park Keeper.

'Run for it.' Shouted out Andrew, the gorilla started making really deep vocal sounds, then Fudge started running on all fours, 'wait, Fudge, don't leave us behind!' shouted Andrew, the big ape suddenly stopped running, huffed and grunted a few times; then went back to get the kids.

Andrew and Gemma climbed onto the gorilla's broad, Silver-back, then the gorilla started running once again.

'Come back here, you little rascals!' shouted the Park Keeper, but Fudge wasn't going to stop.

'Fudge, Fudge,' shouted Andrew, 'climb this tree, Fudge,' the big ape climbed the tree with ease, then he crossed over into another tree. Then the gorilla crossed into another tree; until he was able to leave the park altogether.

'Wow!' said Andrew. 'Hey, Gem, are you okay?'

'Yes, I'm all right.' Said his sister, 'but we better go home now.'

'Definitely,' said Andrew, 'home, home, Fudge,' and the big gorilla took them back to their back garden.

Chapter Fourteen

Old man Ted Reynolds sipped his cup of tea, the teacup clinked and chattered against the saucer; Ted was shaken-up. He looked pale too, and was left feeling dazed and confused.

Ted was sitting in June Davis's living room, trying to recover from his ordeal. 'Yes, you were right, all along, June,' said Ted, 'it was definitely a gorilla. Strange as hell, 'cause this gorilla had a white face, and a black, hairy body.'

'The gorilla I saw looking through my window, had a regular black face,' said June, drinking her cup of tea. 'Maybe there are two gorillas on the loose out there,' she continued.

'One or two, there shouldn't be any gorillas on the loose, scaring people to death,' added Ted. 'When I recovered consciousness, in the early hours of the morning, I called the Police first thing.'

'I bet they didn't believe you, did they?' said June.

'I don't know if they really believed me or not, June,' said Ted, 'the officer said that they would send a car to check it out, that my call has been noted; and that all calls were recorded.'

'But surely the Police have to take it seriously, now,' said June, 'cause I reported it to the police as well; when I saw that big gorilla looking through my window.'

'The police did call me back,' said Ted, 'they said one of their patrols had been driving around the area, but didn't see a gorilla. The officer also said to me that they had checked with any zoos or safari parks in the region and that none of them was missing a gorilla.'

'Well, we didn't imagine it, did we?' continued June, drinking her tea, whilst deep in thought. 'I mean, we couldn't have imagined it, could not have dreamt that we saw a gorilla looking through our bedroom windows, could we?'

Ted added, 'no we didn't dream it, June, we saw it, it's out there, somewhere; and it's on the loose,' said Ted, nervously.

'Well, I don't know what is happening to the world, anymore?' said June. 'But I've got someone from the council, coming round, any day now, to investigate the matter.'

'Big, ugly ape,' said Ted, sipping his tea.

'Let me put my feet up, for a minute,' said Grandad, 'I'm telling ya, love, these animals are wearing me out; feeding them is like doing a workout.' Grandma came into the living room, with two, big mugs of tea, for them both.

'Well, you do insist on keeping those animals of yours,' said Grandma, 'you have to accept the work that comes with them.'

'I know, I know, let's see what's on the box, shall we?' said, Grandad. He turned the TV on, there was an old black and white film on, Grandad didn't feel like watching that, a quiz show, but Grandad wasn't in a quiz kind of mood.

Grandad flicked on the news channel, the local news was on, and a news reporter was standing in a park, talking to a park keeper. Grandad looked at the park, for a few seconds, then suddenly realised, it was THEIR local park, it was called Victoria Park; the park that Grandad took Andrew and Gemma to. 'Here, Joyce, look at this, that's our local park on the news,' said Grandad.

'Oh, yeah, so it is,' replied Grandma.

The reporter on TV said, 'This is Fiona Sutton, reporting from Victoria Park, for Channel 55 News Network; I have the park keeper here with me, his name is Stanley Milton.'

'Stanley, do you think you could tell us all, what you saw and heard, late last night?' said the reporter. The Park Keeper was a short, chubby man, with a bald head on top, and dark hair on each side of his head. He also had a rat-tail moustache, which made him look like a villain from a comedy film.

The Park Keeper stepped-up to the reporter's microphone, and said, 'Well, I was inspecting the main gates of the park, checking the locks, you know, when I thought I heard some voices and laughter coming from inside the park.'

'I made my way along the path, and after a couple of minutes, I saw three figures in the darkness. Although the park was dark, the figures were close enough to the light of one of the park lamps, for me to see them, for a few short seconds.'

'I'm positive, I saw two young children, a boy and a girl, and a gorilla.'

The reporter took the microphone, and said, 'and you're sure it wasn't someone dressed-up in a gorilla costume? You know, like a fancy-dress costume, something like that? A student playing a prank, perhaps?'

Stanley, the 'Parky,' took a deep breath, and stated, 'it was a real Gorilla, I saw its massive bulk, and it started running on all fours, the children were running around; then they got on the back of the gorilla.'

'I saw the gorilla climb a tree, it was the big, old Oak, over there, then it went across, into another tree, then another, and then I lost sight of the three of them, it was very dark.'

The news reporter, Fiona Sutton, took back the microphone, and said to the camera, 'and there you have it, an eyewitness, who says he is sure he saw a gorilla on the loose, and bizarrely, the Park Keeper is sure the gorilla was with two children.'

'Tomorrow, we will bring you a follow-up to this report, because I will be interviewing two local residents, who also claim that they saw a gorilla on the loose. This is Fiona Sutton, for Channel 55 News Network, now back to the studio.'

Grandad turned and looked at Grandma Joyce, then he said, 'it can't be, can it? I wonder?'

'Well, the reporter said it was a gorilla and two children,' said Grandma.

'Where are the children, now?' asked Grandad.

'They're up in their rooms,' answered Grandma Joyce.

'Well, I better check on old Fudge, and double-check that his enclosure is locked up properly,' said Grandad.

'I don't think we should mention this to the kids, just yet,' said Grandma, 'as we don't want anyone knowing about big Fudge, unless they absolutely have to.'

'You're right, love,' said Grandad, 'let's wait and see what we hear about this gorilla business, first.' And then Grandad left the living room to go and check on the enclosures.

Chapter Fifteen

The stars were out, the moon was in its half-moon phase, and the night was still. 'Come on, Gemma, don't take all night,' said Andrew; young Gemma was struggling to put her left trainer on.

'I'm trying, I'm trying,' said Gemma.

'If you undo the laces a bit, you'll find it easier to get your foot in,' said Andrew.

'I've nearly done it,' said Gemma, and with a final push of her foot, her trainer was on. 'Now we're ready,' said Andrew, he said the words like he was a team captain of a football team, talking to his teammates before a match.

Once again, the bedroom door opened quietly, once again, Andrew's head emerged first, he saw that the coast was clear; and then he and his sister crept along the landing.

Andrew pressed his index finger against his lips, indicating to young Gemma to not make a sound. They both stopped and listened at the top of the stairs. Silence. Well, not quite, there was Grandad's snoring that could be heard in the house, but nothing else.

The key was inserted into the back door, Andrew and Gemma looked at each other, they both smiled at one another; then they went outside.

The children stood below the opening to the gorilla's enclosure, 'Fudge, Fudge, come on,' said Gemma, out of the darkness appeared the big ape. When Fudge saw Andrew and Gemma, his eyes lit up; he was clearly happy and excited to see them.

'Look what I've got you, Fudge,' said Andrew, then Andrew placed some Liquorice Allsorts into the large, open hand of the gorilla. The big ape ate them, chewing away, happily.

Then Andrew, as quietly as he could, opened the door to the enclosure. And a few seconds later, the large gorilla walked out on all fours.

Gemma hugged Fudge on one side and Andrew hugged him on the other.

Then Andrew and his sister climbed onto the back of the great ape, 'okay, Fudge,' said Andrew, 'climb, climb, Fudge.' The children gripped on tightly as big Fudge climbed a tree in the back garden, then the ape climbed onto the roof of Andrew's grandparent's house.

'Let's go into town,' said Andrew.

'Why the town?' asked Gemma.

'Because I've never seen the town at night, and it will be good to see it from the rooftops,' replied Andrew. The three of them made their way along the rooftops of houses, before very long, they were close to Victoria Park, once again. Fudge stopped on one of the roofs, and Andrew said, 'look, there's the park, and I can see the park-keeper; he's walking along the path that runs around the inside of the park fence.'

Big Fudge began to head towards the park, but Andrew stopped him,

'No Fudge, we want to go to the town centre, tonight, town, town,' said Andrew. The gorilla understood Andrew and headed along rooftops, which would take them into town.

After a few minutes, the ape and the children came to the end of a busy street, fortunately, there was a large tree for the gorilla to climb into. The tree also connected to the tree on the opposite side of the street, just a short gap to cross, easy enough for a big gorilla.

However, half-way across, Fudge stopped and indicated that he was hungry, he huffed a few short huffing sounds, too. 'I know you're hungry, Fudge,' said Andrew, 'but I don't have any more sweets for you.'

'I don't have any sweets for tonight, either,' said Gemma.

The gorilla looked disappointed, they had come to a stop directly above the road below, there was a traffic light on the road; the light showed red. Just at that moment, a Moped came whirring along the street, it was a pizza delivery scooter.

Big Fudge suddenly caught the smell of the pizzas in the air, he sniffed and sniffed some more; then he started to huff and get excited. The gorilla looked down at the pizza delivery scooter, below, the rider of the Moped was blissfully unaware, that a gorilla and two young children were above him on the branch.

Suddenly, the big ape reached down with his long arm and opened the box at the back of the scooter, he then reached in, and grabbed one of the pizzas, and then lifted it up into the tree.

When Andrew and Gemma saw this, they both laughed out loud, and the delivery rider heard them, he looked up, and to his amazement, saw a big gorilla eating pizza, above him on the branch.

'Ahhhhhh!' shouted the pizza deliveryman, he revved up his moped, and sped away, as fast as he could. Andrew and Gemma were laughing so much, they nearly fell out of the tree; even big Fudge seemed to be laughing, it's difficult to tell with gorillas.

The ape took a big slice of pizza, and started to munch it, he made noises as he ate, that sounded like he was really content. 'This pizza is so nice,' said Gemma.

'Yes, it is, isn't it?' mumbled Andrew, with his mouth full of pizza.

'I love the pineapple and the ham,' said Andrew, 'there's a special name for this flavour pizza, but I can't remember what it is,' continued Andrew. Soon the pizza was finished, and the three adventurers continued into town, via roofs and trees.

Officers Miller and Hedges were on night-duty, in their marked Police car, they were patrolling the town centre, as usual. The two Policemen were kept busier than most, by young tearaways, out playing pranks, or joy-riding; or whatever teenagers get up to these days.

A call came through to them over the police radio, the message said:

'All available units, be advised, a pizza delivery rider has reported seeing a gorilla, close to the town centre. The gorilla stole one of the rider's pizzas, and there are two children with the gorilla, over.'

Police officer Hedges answered the call, as officer Miller was driving, 'yes, that's received, over,' said Officer Miller. 'You know I've just about had enough of this monkey business, lately,' said officer Miller; 'first we get reports from local residents about seeing a gorilla in their back gardens, then the local Parky is giving TV interviews about seeing a gorilla, and now, even a pizza delivery rider, has seen it.'

'We better check it out,' said officer Hedges, and then he turned his siren on and flashing lights.

By now, the gorilla, Andrew and Gemma, were directly above the town's High road. 'Wow, look at the high road at night, Gem, it looks so different from up here,' said Andrew.

'I can see the sweet shop we sometimes go in,' said young Gemma.

'And there's Sainsbury's,' said Andrew, 'let's go down to ground level, and have a look around,' said Andrew. The children held on tight to big Fudge, and then Andrew said, 'down, down, Fudge, take us down.'

The big ape started to climb down, he saw a street lamp within reach of the roof, because of the overhang of the light. Fudge reached across, using one of his large, powerful arms; he just about made it.

Then Fudge reached out with his overarm, and with both hands, held on to the street lamp; while both children held on to the gorilla, tightly. The lamp swayed about a bit, like a tall, thin tree with too much weight on it; but it didn't keel over.

The gorilla climbed down the street lamp, one hand at a time, until they had all reached the ground. There was a cake shop next to the dry cleaners, and big Fudge noticed it straight away.

In the window of the cake shop, was a multi-layered Wedding cake, about two and a half feet high. The ape approached the window and tried to grab the cake, his big hand banged against the windowpane with a thud.

Fudge huffed and grunted a few times, 'no Fudge you can't have that cake,' said Andrew, 'it's not for sale, it's for a wedding too, and you're not getting married.'

The big gorilla indicated that he wanted to eat the cake, by putting his fingers close to his mouth, then he tapped at the window once more. 'No, Fudge we can't get you that c——' Gemma didn't have time to finish her sentence; suddenly they heard a police siren. A couple of seconds later, they saw a police car turn the corner onto the high street.

'Run for it!' shouted Andrew, big Fudge didn't understand what the police car was, or why it was making that racket. As Andrew ran down the high street, he made sure he grabbed his sister's arm, as she was so young, and he didn't want to leave her behind.

The ape then started to run on all fours, he could move quickly, when he wanted to, he soon shot past the kids, huffing and grunting as he did.

'Wait for us!' shouted Andrew. 'Come back here Fudge!' The police car had almost caught up with Andrew and Gemma, Officer Miller put his head out of the side window, and shouted, 'you two, stop right now!'

Officer Miller skidded to a stop, then police officer Hedges jumped out of the other side of the car, 'I've got them,' he said to Officer Miller. When, all of a sudden, a big hairy, black shape ran past him, and scooped up Andrew and his sister; and raced back up the town high street.

'So there is a gorilla on the loose,' said officer Hedges, police officer Miller couldn't believe his eyes, when he saw the gorilla.

'Get back in the car,' shouted officer Miller to officer Hedges, 'We'll head them off.'

Chapter Sixteen

Big Fudge seemed to be running for his life, he didn't like being chased, and he was confused and unsure of what was going on.

The ape ran down the high street with Andrew and Gemma holding on for dear life. 'Andrew I'm scared!' shouted Gemma.

'Just hold on tightly, Gem, we have to get away,' shouted back Andrew. By now, the two officers had done a three-point turn in the road, and were giving chase to the gorilla.

'Get on the radio,' said officer Miller, 'tell the station we need more units in the town centre; we've seen the gorilla and there are two children with it.'

'Right,' said officer Hedges.

The kids and the gorilla could hear the police siren getting louder as it drew nearer to them, they could see the flashing lights of the police car reflected in the windows of the closed shops too.

Fudge reached the end of the high street, he huffed and Andrew shouted, 'down this way, Fudge, hurry.' The gorilla was like a large black blur, running through the shadows thrown out by the street lamps.

'They've gone left, round the corner,' said officer Hedges, 'don't lose them; I'm gonna get the taser-gun ready.'

Big Fudge had made it to another street corner, 'this way Fudge, turn left,' shouted Andrew, the road the ape ran into was an access road, behind one side of the high street.

There was one of those automatically controlled bollards blocking access into the road, it was only open to truck drivers making deliveries. 'Why are we going this way, Andrew?' shouted Gemma.

'Because the police car won't be able to follow us down here!' shouted back Andrew. The big gorilla ran down the access road with Andrew and Gemma still clinging on, desperately. It was a long road, parallel to the high street, Fudge hurried along it, heading for the other end of the road, which was also marked by a bollard.

'We can get out this side, and get away,' said Andrew to his sister and Fudge, but then, suddenly, another police car screeched to a stop, right in front of them.

'Oh no,' shouted out Andrew, big Fudge stopped running and was not sure what to do, or what was going on.

This was a different police car, two new officers got out, one had a taser gun in his hand; this was officer Thorpe, the police officer pointed his taser gun at the gorilla, and shouted: 'Stop right there, don't move!'

'Climb, climb, Fudge,' shouted out Andrew, and so the gorilla jumped up onto a set of Wheelie bins, to his left. Then big Fudge jumped up onto a low-lying roof extension; which enabled him to climb up onto a higher roof, knocking off roof tiles due to his large weight.

The children heard a loud static sound, a sharp, buzzing, electrical sound; Officer Thorpe had discharged his taser gun but had missed the big ape. Then Officer Thorpe was joined by his colleague, Officer Reed.

Within a few seconds, Fudge the gorilla, and the children had made it onto the roof of the high street shops. Officer Reed talked to officers Miller and Hedges, via the police radios, 'this is officer Reed, the gorilla and the kids have gone up onto the roofs of the stores, we want you to drive around back onto the high street; in case they come back down on that side of the street, over.'

'Will do, over,' said officer Hedges on the radio. Fudge moved quickly along the rooftops, trying to find somewhere to go.

'What are we going to do, Andrew?' shouted out young Gemma, then Andrew spotted a lamppost on the high street.

'I know,' said Andrew, 'stop Fudge, stop!' The gorilla came to a sudden stop. 'Down, down, Fudge, take us down, use the lamp post like before,' said Andrew.

Once again, big Fudge reached out from the edge of the roof, stretching as far as he could, then he grabbed the over-hanging light part of the lamp post. This time the gorilla slid down the lamp post, like a fire-fighter sliding down a station pole.

'Yeahhhh!' Fudge, you did it!' shouted out, Andrew.

'You're the greatest, Fudge!' shouted Gemma.

'Okay, let's go, before the police have time to catch up with us,' said Andrew. But the big ape didn't move; he was looking at something in the shop window, directly opposite him.

Fudge had seen a large, cuddly, female soft-toy gorilla in the window of a charity shop, for sale. Big Fudge thought the soft — toy gorilla was a real, alive, one; Fudge seemed to be in love.

'But we have to go, Fudge!' shouted Andrew.

'Stop right there!' said a voice, the voice belonged to a police officer, it was Officer Miller, who had his taser gun pointed at the ape.

Fudge turned to look at the policeman, the ape huffed and grunted, 'don't move a muscle,' said Officer Miller; 'you kids are in trouble.' Suddenly, big Fudge jumped back up the lamp post, with a big leap, officer Miller fired his taser gun; the electric barb struck the lamp post, missing the gorilla by a few inches.

The electric shock was instantaneous, Officer Miller had inadvertently electrocuted himself, the police officer cried out in pain, 'Ahhh!' Officer Miller dropped his taser gun, and fell to the pavement. At that same moment, Fudge jumped back up onto the roofs of the shops, and ran along the rooftops on all fours.

Officer Hedges had just arrived on the scene when the ape and the kids escaped again. The police officer rushed over to assist his injured colleague, 'are you okay, mate?' asked officer Hedges, Officer Miller was just starting to recover from the electric shock, but couldn't speak.

The radio on officer Hedges uniform crackled into life, a voice over the radio said, 'can you see the gorilla, over?' It was Officer Thorpe, officer Hedges replied. 'Officer Miller is down; he seems to have injured himself with his own taser. I can't see the gorilla, or the children, they may be back up on the roofs, over,'

'Roger that, I'm calling in the dog unit to assist us; the K-9 will be able to pick up the gorilla's scent, over,' said Officer Thorpe. While Officer Thorpe was talking on his radio, big Fudge the gorilla was running along the high street shop's roofs.

Fudge reached the end of the high street, there was a tree on the pavement below, fortunately, its branches reached across far enough for the ape to climb out onto.

The gorilla moved through the tree, with the children holding on, the ape knuckle-walked out onto a branch on the over-side of the tree. The big gorilla swung with one massive arm holding a branch, and grabbed a branch with his other hand; this branch belonged to a tree directly opposite the first tree.

By doing this, Fudge and the children had been able to cross the high street, without descending to the ground. A police car siren could now be heard, approaching the town centre, Andrew said to the gorilla, 'Fudge, take us to the park, hurry.'

The ape ran on all fours, this time on the other side of the high street roofs. The ape reached the end of the street, once again, there was a tree for the gorilla to climb on to, but there wasn't a tree on the opposite side.

'You have to climb down the tree, Fudge,' said Andrew. Fudge climbed down the tree in a matter of seconds; then he headed across the road, to a tree on a street corner.

Police car sirens grew louder, voices behind the gorilla could be heard in the darkness. Car headlights picked out the gorilla as it climbed another tree. Officers Thorpe and Reed rushed along in their marked police car, 'I saw them running along the shop roofs, on the other side of the high street,' said Officer Reed.

Police officer Thorpe was driving, officer Reed looked in the glove compartment for a torch, 'I'm gonna grab a torch, we're gonna need one,' said Officer Reed.

By now, the police car was just about directly beneath big Fudge's position on the road below.

'I can see the gorilla and the two kids,' said Officer Reed.

'They are probably heading for the park; it's at the end of this road,' said Officer Thorpe, excitedly.

The police car came to the junction at the end of the road, opposite the park, officer Reed flashed his torch around, the bright beam of white light danced around. The light bounced off windows and roofs, then Officer Reed shone the torchlight into the branches of a tree, that stretched out, over the park fence.

'I just saw the ape!' shouted Officer Reed, 'they're in the park!' Just then another police car siren could be heard approaching the park, from another direction.

Big Fudge clambered through the branches of trees, breaking many of the smaller ones he touched, but as long as he kept his body weight on the larger ones, he wouldn't fall.

'Stop Fudge!' shouted Andrew, 'take us back down again!'

'No Andrew,' said Gemma, who was scared, 'if we stay up in the trees, they can't catch us.'

'No Gemma,' replied Andrew, 'if we go back down onto the path, we can move much quicker; we can run to the other side of the park, before the police have time to get into the park.'

'Down Fudge, down,' said Andrew, the ape reached out with both arms, wrapping his arms around the trunk of the tree, like he was hugging it. Then the gorilla allowed himself to slide down the trunk, to the ground.

It was at that moment, that the gorilla and the children, heard a dog barking. Andrew and Gemma both knew instantly that it was the police and they were in the park.

The police dog unit was on the scene now, police officer Johnson with his German Shepard, 'Shuttle,' because he was a fast dog.

Officer Johnson had been quickly briefed, by the other police officers outside the police gates. Officer Johnson had already lifted his dog over the Park railings, and was now climbing over the railings himself. The German Shepherd was barking excitedly, but didn't go running off into the park, just yet; it was too well trained for that, it waited for its handler to be ready.

Big Fudge, with the kids holding on, ran on all fours along the park pathway. By now, there was more and more barking, and it was getting closer. Andrew looked behind him, he could see a torchlight bouncing around in the darkness. 'Hurry Fudge, we don't want to get caught,' said Andrew, the gorilla grunted back, he was fully aware of the danger.

On the outskirts of the park, through the trees, a police car's flashing light could be seen, bright red and blue flashes of colour. The gorilla was coming up to the end of the park pathway, Andrew heard the police dog approaching, quickly. 'Climb the park gate, Fudge, hurry!' shouted Andrew. Fudge began to climb the large, heavy green painted gate.

As the gorilla climbed to the top of the gate, the police dog arrived and jumped up and tried to bite the backside of big Fudge. The dog was barking like mad, too; it was desperate to bite and hold on, but luckily for Andrew and Gemma, big Fudge had made it over the park gate.

The police car sped towards the park gate. It was Officers Thorpe and Reed, but the children saw it approaching, Andrew said, 'let's keep to the pavement, we can use the parked cars as cover.' The big ape ran on all fours along the pavement, and the police officers couldn't see him.

Police Officer Johnson had reached the park gate, and got control of his dog, he was talking to the other police officers through the park gate.

Andrew saw his chance, 'if we run across the road to that big tree, over there, we can climb that tree and get on to the roof of that house. Then we can run along the roofs and get back home', said Andrew.

'Go Fudge.' Said Andrew, 'tree, tree,' the gorilla ran on all fours across the dark road, he reached the base of a large tree and started to climb it.

At that moment, the German Shepherd dog started barking again and straining at the leash. 'He's got the scent again,' said Officer Johnson to the other officers, 'come on! The gorilla must have gone up this way.'

It took a few seconds for Officer Johnson to lift his dog over the park railings, and then climb over himself. But they were at the base of the tree in no time, with the German Shepherd with his two front legs on the tree trunk, looking up at the branches, barking.

'Kick the torchlight on the tree,' said one of the officers, the bright light waved about like a giant Light-Saber. Then the light captured the ape and the kids moving about on one of the branches above.

'There they are!' shouted Police Officer Hedges. 'Stop right there, you're in trouble!' he shouted out, but all Andrew could think of was escaping.

'Keep going Fudge, get on the roof of the house, quick, quick,' Andrew said.

Now Fudge was up on the roof of yet another house. He began to knuckle walk at a fast pace, keeping his substantial bodyweight on the top of the roofs.

Although the children could hear police sirens on the streets below and the police dog barking, just a few short minutes and they were back in their own garden.

The kids couldn't believe that they had gotten away from the police, but they had.

Big Fudge the gorilla sat down on the lawn in an upright position. He was breathing heavily from all his excursions.

Andrew and Gemma sat down next to Fudge. 'That tired me out,' said Andrew, 'I didn't think we'd be chased by the Police.'

'Why did the Police chase us, anyway, Andrew?' asked young Gemma.

'You know what, I don't know why? Maybe they just don't like gorillas?' answered Andrew.

'I don't know how anyone couldn't like you, Fudge?' said Gemma, and then she hugged the big ape.

'Yeah, you're the best, Fudge,' said Andrew and he hugged big Fudge too.

Then the large gorilla wrapped his big arms around the kids and hugged them back. Fudge huffed a few times and the children knew the gorilla was telling them that he liked them, too, in his own unique way.

Chapter Seventeen

The next morning was a bright and sunny one. Sunlight shone into the living room of Grandad and Grandma's home. Grandad and Grandma were both drinking tea while sitting on their sofa in the living room. Andrew and his sister walked in, half asleep; after all, they had had a very eventful night.

'Morning, you two,' said Grandma. The children sat down on the armchairs in the living room.

'Morning Grandma, morning Grandad,' replied Andrew and Gemma together.

'Sleepy, are we?' said Grandad.

'Mmm,' mumbled Andrew, looking at his grandparents, 'I do feel tired today.'

'Late night, was it?' asked their grandma. Gemma looked over at Andrew, who shot a quick glance at Gemma.

'What do you mean, Grandma?' asked Andrew, enquiringly.

'I think you two little scamps should level with us, don't you?' said their grandad.

'Sorry Grandad, what do you mean?'

'Well, we know that a certain couple of children around here have been getting up to all sorts of mischief, don't we, Joyce?' said Grandad.

'Oh, yes we do,' said Grandma, 'a certain boy and girl, not a million miles from here, have been playing around at night with a gorilla.'

'How did you know, Grandma?' asked Andrew, surprised that the game was up.

'Well...'

'We know about your little antics,' interrupted Grandad, 'because our neighbours are talking about seeing two children and a gorilla at night and, so is the TV news!'

'And just how many gorillas and two children live around here, eh?' said their grandma.

'But why didn't you tell us that you had a gorilla, Grandad?' enquired Andrew, amazed.

'More to the point, why were you two out so late at night when you should have been at home sleeping?' asked their grandad.

'We couldn't help it, Grandad,' said Gemma, 'we just wanted to play with Fudge.'

'You two are too young to be out so late at night,' said their grandma.

'I'm sorry Grandma, er, I mean, we're sorry. We were only having fun with the gorilla, we were only playing,' said Andrew.

'Well, that may be, but you have caused quite a ruckus around these parts,' answered Grandad.

'You've been scaring the neighbours to death,' said their grandma, 'and by the sounds of it, giving the police the run around as well.'

'But we didn't mean to be chased by the police, Grandma,' said Andrew. 'We didn't do anything wrong. We just wanted to go out and play with Big Fudge, and suddenly, the police started chasing us!'

'Yes, but you two little tykes shouldn't have been out that late, running around town, especially with a big Silverback gorilla!' said the children's grandmother, rather sternly.

'We're sorry, Grandma,' said young Gemma, again, 'but when we saw Fudge in his enclosure, all alone, we just wanted to give him some space and friendship; we just wanted to have fun together, that's all.'

'Fudge is our friend, now,' shouted Andrew, 'we love the gorilla; he looked after us.'

'And we eat sweets together,' revealed Gemma.

'Oh, do you now?' said their grandad. 'Well, although we don't approve of you two young ones being out so late at night, we can understand you two liking big old Fudge so much. After all, Your grandma and I love that big, old, soppy thing.'

'But Grandad,' said Andrew, 'you told us all about your other animals in your menagerie, but why didn't you tell us you had a gorilla, as well?' asked Andrew.

'Well,' said Grandad, 'it is about time I told you the full story, I suppose. I have a friend who used to be a zookeeper at a zoo about a hundred miles from here. And, this zoo was only a small zoo that was not very popular, probably because of the way the zoo was run.' Grandad continued, 'this zoo didn't have many animals and it was going out of business; the owners of the zoo had to find zoos and safari parks that would take their animals and give them a new home.' Andrew and Gemma listened with much interest as their grandad continued with his story.

'The problem was they couldn't find a zoo or safari park that would take a baby gorilla; they were already full or didn't have the facilities for keeping a gorilla. Well, after trying to find somewhere that would take the baby gorilla and not being successful, my friend, the zookeeper, remembered me.'

'He knew I really liked animals and that I have a menagerie, so he called me and we arranged for me to drive up there and see the baby gorilla.'

'A few days later, I arrived at the zoo and met baby Fudge. And that reminds me,' continued Grandad, 'if you're wondering how Fudge got his name, it's because when I first met the baby gorilla, I was eating a packet of fudge and so I thought it would make a good name for him.'

'And when I met the little gorilla, I must admit I fell in love with him and said that I would give him a home and take good care of him.'

'But I didn't have a licence to keep a gorilla in my menagerie so I had to keep it quiet, you see, and that's why your grandmother and I didn't tell anyone, including you two.'

'We're sorry, Grandad, we didn't know you didn't have a licence to keep a gorilla,' said Andrew.

'Yes, well now, half the neighbourhood know about our gorilla,' said Grandad. Just at that moment, they all heard a vehicle pull-up outside their house.

Gemma rushed over to the window and said, 'There's a van outside, Grandma.'

Everyone in the living room went to the window to look outside. The van had the words 'ENVIRONMENTAL HEALTH OFFICER' on the side of it.

Grandad's eyes opened wide in shock, 'quick, quick, we've got to hide Fudge!' he exclaimed. 'Kids, you have to help me out the back; Joyce, you're going to have to stall him. Offer him a slice of one of your cakes and a cup of tea,' said Grandad.

Grandad, Andrew and Gemma hurried towards the back door. Grandad grabbed the key and as he did so, turned and said to Joyce, 'whatever you do, don't let that man into the back garden until we're ready!'

'Okay, I won't,' replied Grandma. As Grandad and the kids disappeared out the back door, the front doorbell rang. Grandma composed herself and then took her time before opening the front door.

The man on the doorstep said, 'Good morning, Madam. I'm an Environmental Health Officer from the Council. I'm here to inspect the animals in your menagerie.'

'What are we going to do Grandad?' asked Andrew, anxiously.

'I'm thinking, I'm thinking,' said their grandad. 'Maybe I could put Fudge in with Bruce, the Red River Hog,' said Grandad to the children. 'No, on the other hand, the man from the Council is bound to check in all the enclosures.'

'What about hiding Fudge in the tree, Grandad?' said Gemma. The kid's Grandad looked at the tree, then realised it wouldn't work. 'No, Fudge would still be seen,' he said.

Then Grandad looked at the upstairs windows of his house and had an idea.

'Quick! Kids, help me get the ladder out of the shed.' Grandad rushed over to his garden shed and unlocked the door to the shed; tins of paint and boxes fell out.

Then, Grandad saw the ladder on top of a stack of boxes near the top of the shed. 'Hurry! We don't have much time,' said Grandad as he pulled the step ladder out.

'Your cake is delicious Mrs Tyler,' said the man from the Council, 'It tastes so much better than the cakes I buy from the supermarket and, I must admit, I do like a nice cup of tea with a slice of cake.'

'Oh, I am pleased you like it. I do like to bake cakes and it's nice to get some positive comments regarding my baking.'

Grandma Joyce poured the man some more tea. As she did so, the man from the Council said, 'Do you think your husband will be ready soon?'

'Yes, Alex is just finishing feeding his animals; he shouldn't be much longer,' said Grandma Joyce.

Just then, young Andrew came rushing into the house and ran upstairs to his bedroom. As he hurried upstairs, Grandma called out to him, 'Andrew, has Grandad finished feeding his animals yet?'

'Er, not quite yet, Grandma, but almost,' replied Andrew. Then they heard Andrew's bedroom door open and close.

Grandma Joyce looked at the man from the Council and said, 'Kids, eh?'

In his bedroom, Andrew opened his bedroom window. He saw the ladder just below the window sill, then he said, 'Okay, Grandad, I'm ready.'

'Great,' said Grandad, 'Now grab hold of the top of the ladder and hold on for dear life, I'm gonna have to do this quickly.'

Grandad went and unlocked the door to Fudge's enclosure. 'Fudge, Fudge,' said Grandad, 'I need you to come with me, big boy. Otherwise, you're gonna get discovered and taken off me.'

'Quickly, Fudge, this way,' said Grandad. Big Fudge followed Grandad to the base of the ladder. 'Andrew, I need you to call Fudge up to you,' said Grandad.

'Okay, Grandad,' said Andrew. 'Fudge, up here, Fudge, climb up here, Fudge!' said Andrew, eagerly. The big gorilla sniffed the air, huffed, and then began to climb the ladder.

The step ladder began to strain under the weight of the big ape. 'We have to hold the ladder in place,' said Grandad. 'Gemma, help me.'

Slowly, but surely, big Fudge climbed up the ladder towards Andrew. 'Good boy, Fudge,' said Andrew, 'keep going, you can do it.' After a few seconds, which seemed like minutes, big Fudge was at Andrew's window. Andrew hugged his large, hairy friend. 'It's so good to see you again, Fudge,' said Andrew.

'I need you to hide in my room for a while, Fudge,' said Andrew, hoping that the gorilla would, somehow, understand.

Andrew took hold of the ape's hands and tried to help the gorilla get through the open window, but big, old Fudge got stuck; he was too big for the opening. Andrew pulled Fudge's arms, this helped a little, but the big gorilla was still stuck.

'Grandad, Grandad,' said Andrew, 'Fudge is stuck, I need help!'

'Okay, okay, I hear you. I'm going to climb up and push Fudge while you pull him,' said Grandad. Grandad began to climb the ladder. 'Gemma, I need you to hold the bottom of the ladder for me, okay?'

'Yes, Grandad, I'll try,' said young Gemma. Their grandad reached the place on the ladder where the gorilla was. He started to push Fudge; Grandad pushed with all his strength and Andrew pulled Fudge with all his strength.

'Fudge is moving a bit, Grandad,' said Andrew.

'That's good to hear,' replied Grandad, 'keep pulling, will you?' Andrew continued to pull the big ape's arms and Grandad pushed and pushed. Then, finally, after a big struggle, big Fudge went through the open window and collapsed onto the bedroom floor with a loud thud.

Downstairs, the man from the Council looked up at the ceiling after hearing a loud, crashing noise upstairs. Grandma looked at him; then, the man said 'I know, kids, eh?'

A couple of minutes later Grandad walked into the living room and said, 'Those animals are wearing me out; they really are.'

Andrew had pulled the curtains in his bedroom halfway across and he, Gemma and big Fudge were watching out the bedroom window, secretly.

They watched Grandad show the Environmental Health Officer around the menagerie. They saw the man from the Council ticking boxes on a checklist on his clipboard.

The man checked every enclosure in turn and seemed satisfied by the time he left. Big Fudge huffed deeply, like a good gorilla does. His breath steamed up the windowpane.

A minute after the man from the Council left, Grandad and Grandma came into Andrew's bedroom. By now, Andrew, Gemma and Fudge were all sitting on the bed. 'Is everything alright, Grandad?' asked Andrew.

'That was a close call,' answered Grandad. 'I hope I don't go through that again.'

'We did it!' shouted Andrew. 'We kept our gorilla a secret!'

'I don't know how?' said their grandma.

'Now, we can have much more fun!' said Gemma.

'Much more fun?' said Grandad. 'I need a holiday from you two kids and that big, hairy gorilla.'

Andrew and Gemma hugged Fudge. 'Our fun is just beginning,' said Andrew.

'Yeahhhh!' said Gemma.

'We're going to have lots more adventures together,' said Andrew.

'Heaven help us!' said their grandad. And big Fudge just huffed a couple of times, you know, like gorillas do.

The End